Y0-BOC-085

In Memoriam

We wish to remember those close who have succumbed recently.

Patricia Durel Vassar	1909-1988
Charles H. Brown	1906-1989
John E. Field	1910-1961
Edwin E. Brown	1907-1961

Each of them, my sister, husband and brother-in-law and old time friend, were raised here in the Ross Valley, contributing in their own way to many of the stories herein.

We would like to give thanks to the following for use of their historical photos, many of them rare and unpublished:

Roy Farrington Jones

Mary Ellen Ball

Jack Farley

Alan Moder

Dick and Jayne Murdock

Marty Marcucci

and The San Anselmo Historical Commission
(Sharon Deveaux, Laurie Smith and Karen Liberatore)

San Anselmo Public Library
110 Tunstead Avenue
San Anselmo, CA 94960

SAN ANSELMO LIBRARY

3 1111 02223 3199

DISCARDED

*T*racks from the *J*unction

Historical Anecdotes of San Anselmo & Ross Valley

Larine Brown

Marin Light Press
San Anselmo, CA

Copyright © Larine Brown, 1992

All rights reserved. No part of this book may be reproduced in any form or by any means without permission in writing from the Publisher, Marin Light Press, 81 Elm Ave., San Anselmo, CA 94960

Book design and production by Janet Andrews
Desktop Studio, Larkspur, CA

Library of Congress Catalog Card No.: 92-80275
ISBN 0-9632390-0-7
Printed in the United States of America

Preface

San Anselmo has its heritage of hills where the eye may roam in contemplation and atop it all in the distance is added the figure of Mt. Tamalpais. God speaks of this in His scriptures, and theologians elected it as an appropriate setting for an international seminary.

Many retreats of various faiths, as well as churches, found an idyllic setting here. Lifelong residents found more than aestheticism—a solemn union to the Divine. Fleeting faiths may come and go but this American town sends its clarion bells to welcome the true pilgrims.

> "I lift mine eyes to the hills.
> From whence does my help come?
> My help comes from the Lord
> Who made heaven and earth."
>
> —Psalm 121: 1 and 2

Introduction

These stories contain my memories of those I know who live or have lived in San Anselmo and environs during my growing up years.

Of a pioneer family of the Pacific northwest I arrived in the Ross-Kentfield area with my family many years ago. My dad, Ned O'Brien, was a Pacific maritime hero, dying young from injuries suffered while trying to rescue a ship in the Bering Sea.

Mother, Agnes, became Marin's first lady journalist in 1921 as editor on the San Anselmo Herald on Tunstead Avenue here. My news writing career began in 1936 when as a teen-ager I became a cub reporter on the 100-year old Marin Journal, the state's oldest weekly.

Charles Brown a native San Anselman and I were married in 1940 raising our three children in this town. We became the proud grandparents of seven before Charles, a state building supervisor succumbed to Lew Gehrig's disease in 1989. I consistently wrote for the county papers except for the period in southern California where my husband was supervising construction of state buildings at San Luis Obispo and Long Beach.

These stories have previously been published in the column *Tracks from the Junction* in the *Ross Valley Reporter*, one of the Marinscope papers.

San Anselmo

San Anselmo is my home town
Where I'm known if not renown.
Where the people on the street
Happily stop to greet.

Mt. Tamalpais is looking over
The sleeping maid lays in the clover
Through the years of changing scene
Seminary spires are supreme.

Fitted in the hills so neat
Making tourists feel complete
Beauty through the Ross Valley
Real Estate is a rally.

San Anselmo has it all.
Hub, of the great recall.

—Larine O'Brien Brown
2-27-88

San Anselmo, 1887. The road is Sir Francis Drake Boulevard. From left to right is Seminary Hill, Milanis Vineyard, Bald Hill, tracks to Fairfax, and tracks to San Rafael. Roy Farrington Jones Private Collection.

An Artistic View

Ever since I was asked to write a column about the area, I've had many anecdotes come to the fore.

Our family came into Kentfield from Seattle in 1921, and mother was a first newswoman on the old San Anselmo Herald.

As a child, I would come from Ross School into the Herald office on Tunstead Avenue, sit on a stool and write on a pad of paper while waiting for Mom to go home. At a tender age, I grew to love the veritable smell of printer's ink, get to know newspeople and like them.

San Anselmo was like the big city, as we traveled the train from our home on Kent Avenue. The restaurants and movies were there and lots of my friends.

Next door to the news office was Arthur Shearer's Plumbing, across the street from the San Anselmo Library that stands today. Tom Minto owned the original building, still present. Old photos show the Tin Lizzies parked in front.

The residents then liked to hark back to war days or the turn of the century. Most old-timers were impressed by the brazen bank robber, arriving on horseback to hold up the First Bank of San Anselmo, corner of Bank Street and Sir Francis Drake Boulevard. He filled his saddlebags and made a hasty getaway, though many gun-toting lookers-on took pot shots at him. And a train had arrived across the street and riders observed the Wild West firsthand. George Martin, the only policeman, missed him, too.

Highlights of San Anselmo History

Our first indications of the town's name come from papers of the Punta de Quintin grant of 1840, namely Canada de Anselmo. Canada (valley) was probably named for a baptized Indian and the

San added later. The present name was applied to the North Pacific Coast Railroad station in the 1890's. In 1874 the railroad added spur track from San Anselmo to San Rafael and in 1875 completed the line from Sausalito to Tomales via San Anselmo. In 1883 the town was renamed San Anselmo after being called Junction since 1875.

First Home

High atop a knoll in Sequoia Park stands the George Lucas Victorian home that was originally built in 1869 by Minthorne Tompkins for his large family upon arriving in the area. Minthorne owned all of Sequoia Park, then a ranch of 150 acres, sold it to a developer, Mr. Doughty, who later sold it back to the original owner. The top story was at one time sold off but later returned when Mr. Lucas had restoration done which included many skylights through the home. The Tompkins daughter, Miss Ethel Tompkins organized the Marin Humane Society in 1907.

Did you need a quick change of scenery on a hot summer day? Jump into your Cad or Toyota and roll it down some of the Valley's cooler streets. Shady Lane in Ross, that historical avenue of Elms (some of which have been removed) or go down Ross Avenue in San Anselmo, keeping to the back roads by the Branson School and on the Lake Phoenix area by the Lagunitas Tennis Club in Ross. You'll soon see why there were adamant conservators of trees in Marin. The end of Cascade Drive in Fairfax can hold a candle to all of them. (They wonder why Marin is beautiful). It's the trees that make the difference. Murray Park in Kentfield is a cool, neat drive not far away and no freeway travel. These are mini-trips one might enjoy.

†⚬†

Promoters of the Ross Valley have come and gone—but the beauty and weather remain its greatest attraction. It's been described by writers, artists and musicians—attracting also those needing health improvement.

Like a vintage wine, memories of those days are softened as we recall figures on the stage of life. Always the beautiful backdrops of just pure beauty in nature.

In that day, dishonesty in public office shocked the public. The

William Deysher case was uppermost. Deysher was an auto dealer of great popularity—and even after the findings of underhanded dealings and his consequent arrest, his loyal friends never let him down.

What makes the Ross Valley what it is? The back roads on which you could learn to drive freeways? The bumper-to-bumper traffic on Sir Francis Drake at 5 p.m.? No—just the jockeying into your own driveway to look over green hills. The greens, bushes, trees, lawns, show an artistic view from any angle.

The Sherrick house on Elm Avenue is a personal memorial to Mr. and Mrs. Sam Sherrick, who lived there years ago. Occupied by many others since, those who grew up around there always remembered Mrs. Sherrick, a childless woman with a great love for all the children. She spent her days being another mother to the needs of the kids.

ooooo

The old vehicles tell the story of real estate row in San Anselmo. A booming business when property was sold rapidly and cheap to San Franciscans. Mary Ellen Ball Collection.

Nothing Untold

As I peruse the old journals and papers in my search for appropriate material, I find it strange when I come across some of my own and my mother's writings that have been published since 1921.

Agnes O'Brien was a Marin journalist for 15 years before she suffered a stroke at her editor's desk on the old Marin Journal. After her demise a neophyte was launched into the incredibly fascinating work of recording Marin history ... namely me, at that time a 19-year-old Larine A. O'Brien raised in the newspaper atmosphere with nary a course in journalism.

How did I do it? 1 fell into it like a natural. Many friends from Ross where I grew up kept me supplied with news and with some basic ability with sentence structure I made out just fine. I recorded my history as well as the county's and managed to stir up the competitors to a frenzy that never did slow down.

First Lady Mayor

No one could forget Carmel Booth, the first woman to be elected mayor of San Anselmo in 1948. She believed herself to be a vociferous mixture of Jewish and Irish and many compared her to Carmen of the opera. There was just no middle course for Carmel, and many a session of her forthright speeches caused near apoplexy to visiting dignitaries. One such from the fraud division of the IRS had such a blood pressure reaction from Carmel's outspoken manner, he had to leave the meeting. Carmel did not mince words about realtor's row but instead called it robber's row. She and her husband later moved to Lakeport where she waged an active war on ridding Clear Lake of bugs, etc. She became a secretary to their local board. Her picturesque speech left nothing untold and she left many friends among the citizenry.

In those days (we're talking about yesteryear) everyone hiked. In San Anselmo the closest available place was Mt. Baldy, so that's where most people went. No TV then, no VCR to rent movies for—just get out and walk and enjoy the out-of-doors and gaze at nature.

One prominent gentleman of the town enjoyed it all to the extent that he should have joined a nudist camp. There was a group of kids who decided to investigate what was going on at the top of Mt. Baldy. They found out … much to the chagrin of all, and that was the end of his sun bathing spree au naturale.

Huck Finns

One hot summer day back in 1928 two Kentfield boys decided to take a canoe ride out in San Francisco Bay. Jack Field and Mick O'Brien left Ross, taking the latter's dog "Wager," leaving from their Escalle "port." Mid-bay the canoe turned over and a long swim for the boys (luckily both good swimmers) brought them into the track of the old ferry slip piling. "Wager" was on Mick's head (he wasn't going to leave his dog behind). Today these former boys are still good friends. Jack's father Harry was the station master at Ross. The two Victorians restored and made into shopping areas in Ross, belonged to his parents and grandparents, pioneers of the area. Mick graduated from all the local schools, matriculated at U.C. of Davis and after war-time duty joined a partnership in sheep and rice farming in Williams, Colusa Co. Jack was always a water lover and Mick, born at Puget Sound, had a sea-faring father and grandfather.

Great Fiasco

Remember when Cal Trans decided they were going to place Highway 17 in Sleepy Hollow thence on to Terra Linda and/or vice versa? The hue and cry of the citizens was strong enough to form many homeowner's associations through the valley. These had not existed before and fight they did to annihilate the plan. Vera Rivers, realtor and public speaker, was a standout in the drive and spearheaded the campaign to stop the proposed highway. Mrs. Rivers, 88, who lived at the Nazareth House in San Rafael passed away last year.

Tamsel Brown Hug

We have a picture of Tamsel and her lovely long curls standing in an upstairs window of her family home in Kentfield. She was practicing her violin. The kids wanted her to come out and play, but she couldn't because of practicing. Her hair was of a golden brown shade, very beautiful, and for that she was selected as a choice for the queen of the May dance at Ross School in 1928. Tamsel is now Mrs. Charles Hug, a recent widow, residing in San Anselmo where her sons and grandchildren live.

ooooo

Lansdale Station Crossing near Cullens grocery store about 1912. Alan Moder Collection.

Summers in Marin

Summers in Marin were always lots of fun because it was real country then without so much of the building subdivisions. Kent Woodlands didn't exist back in the 20's and much of the land still belonged to the Kent family.

Anyway, here are further adventures of Jack Field and Mick O'Brien, the two little Ross schoolboys.

Beginning from our house on Kent Avenue, they would hike as far up into the hills as they could go, avoiding the general run of kids playing down below. They first established the "fort" that I, as kid sister, was privileged to see. Later they cut down some trees and made themselves a log cabin with bunks and all in it. What marvelous freedom there was. Our parents knew one another and trusted us. The boys were Scout trained, prepared for emergencies and totally capable even then. No weighty problems. Just fun. Of course there was the case of chickens being found in the Ross Post Office the day after Halloween. Wonder who did that? No, they didn't.

Among the figures of yesteryear that comes to the mind of many is the late Phil Cullens, a staunch little Irishman with a brogue and a kindly heart. He bought out the Lansdale grocery back in 1919 after selling out his Lagunitas Store. During the depression years his generosity and feeling for people saved many from starvation as he kept long charge accounts which were often not paid. His son, Phil Jr. also now deceased, was a University of Santa Clara grad and served San Anselmo as a city councilman.

Our Good Neighbors
The Kentfield postmistress was Mrs. Coleman and her son, Sidney

married Bernice (Bea) Yeo of the William Yeo family. Sid and Bea also worked at the Kentfield P.O. and now live in Petaluma where they have great-grandchildren. At one time the William Yeos had a horse ranch in Sleepy Hollow. He was a contractor of many homes in the area.

Sandlot ball was made more exciting by Bob Keene's father, who supplied all the trappings for baseball and football. Bob still lives in the family home there. His mother, Edith Keene, passed on last year at the age of 90.

Antique Pipes

USA was written in large letters of red, white and blue, very patriotic, on various streets of the city, around the Fourth of July. In the form of large arrows it became increasingly puzzling during this flag burning period, when you would be surprised at such a display.

However, it wasn't long before they found out what USA, pointing in different directions, did mean; it was part of a plan to dig up water pipes dating back to 1903. Galvanized pipes can hold out a long time, but still there comes a time when anything gives away. So if you see the signs, it's not because the kids have been waxing patriotic with hieroglyphics. The letters USA represented places to telephone for the construction foremen.

Julia Child

Julia Child in the wine country! Bon Appetit! Can't you just hear it as she examines the northern California wines. Their affinity and use in the exquisite gourmet meals she displays on television and describes in her best selling books are well known to us all.

She was a local girl too. Educated right up in the Ross hills, at Katharine Branson School during the 30's, having come in from Cambridge, Mass.

Julia, with husband Paul, was just in the area with her sister, Dorothy Cousins, of Sausalito. She has a new book coming out in November entitled, *The Way To Cook*, number one of a two-part series. No doubt to be on a best seller-list soon.

She was Julia McWilliams when she graduated from the Ross girl's school in 1930 where she was a Blue Team Captain and Senior

Marshal. She graduated from Smith College in 1934 and then joined the Office of Strategic Services, meeting Paul Child while both were on assignment in Ceylon and then China. Following their marriage they lived in Paris where Julia studied at the Cordon Bleu with Max Bugnard, who had worked under Escoffier, which led to her lifetime interest in cooking. Two French friends persuaded her to join them in publishing a cookbook for Americans. Ten years later, *Mastering the Art of French Cooking* was published by A. Knopf. Following Mr. Childs' retirement, he joined his wife's successful endeavors after their move to Cambridge where their permanent home is. Summers they spend in Montecito near Santa Barbara while visiting friends in the area.

This unusual culinary teacher was honored by KBS in 1980 with a distinguished alumni award.

The Young Estate

I've been thinking back about the George Young mansion and estate situated across from the Ross School and the train station. It was often used as a setting for moving pictures and Hollywood stars to perform. We received permission to view some child actors on their "stage," which was the lovely green lawn of the Young estate. The beautiful children with golden curls traipsed around in bare feet. I wondered what protected them until I saw them remove strips of adhesive following their rehearsals. It was like a beautiful dream. The gorgeous setting and cute children as central figures.

Moved Away

When Roy Olsen and his wife Nancy moved from San Anselmo Avenue up to Petaluma recently, two people left who have roots here.

Nancy is the daughter of Mrs. Juanita Hubber Finn, of San Rafael, who is a native of San Anselmo and the late Bob Finn of the Mill Valley family by that name.

The couple has six married offspring and many grandchildren. With them was Roy's mother, Eva Valesquez, 88, a San Rafael pioneer.

ooooo

*The Jonathan Kittle home and grounds were purchased by a group of philan-
thropists organized by Mrs. Norman Livermore. Later it become the public
cultural center now known as the Marin Art and Garden Center, Ross. Roy
Farrington Jones Private Library.*

Nellie the Mare

This one's about Nellie, the old brown mare that a Mr. Molenkamp, keeper at Lake Phoenix, owned. He "farmed" her out to neighboring boys, one of whom was this Huck Finn character of the Bay episode, by name of Mick O'Brien in Kentfield.

Nellie kicked the slats out of the old wooden garage next to our house. She decided to chase me around the yard and up my back steps with ears pinned back. She meant business. Sister, Pat, was coaxed to sit on her and her screams of fright were heard far, as there was no telling what that horse would do.

Later in life I heard of a San Anselmo boy, Ed Brown, who had cared for Nellie. He was later to become my brother-in-law, an avid horseman and roper and captain of the Marin Mounted Sheriff's Posse.

October in August

Any day now the work begins by about 65 women on the articles for the Christmas Decor sale to be held in October at the Marin Art and Garden Center, in Ross.

The Decorations building is the center for the artistic greens formations made by the various members and put up for sale at most reasonble prices. Unbelievable prices are now on many of the hand-made articles currently on display, handcarvings of animals, too, that now get exorbitant prices, at specialty stores.

All of this floral creativity began eons ago during the day of the town's founder, James Ross. His grand-daughters, the Worn sisters, daughters of George Worn, who succeeded Ross in ownership of the estate, were heavily into flowers, decorating for the Cotillions and debutante balls in San Francisco. Don Perry, late owner of Sunnyside Nursery, a nephew of the Worns, came by it naturally, too.

Sara Tuckey

Mrs. Robert (Sara) Tuckey, of Kentfield, was the first president of the Garden Society of Marin in 1947 which met at the old pump house on the grounds of the Marin Art and Garden Center.

The-86-year old floral pioneer journeys all over the state giving her expertise in the growing of the flora. Acting as a judge for the various fairs, etc., she, with other's equally qualified, travels on a circuit viewing the various exhibits. She just came from a judging at Turlock.

Along with seven clubs, Mrs. Tuckey's club was one of the original planters of the grounds for Guide Dogs for the Blind, which included herbs for the blind to touch, further enhancing their ability to smell the aromas. She originated the Peacock Gap Garden Club in 1964 and is a lifelong honorary member. Back in 1949 she attended a meeting at the St. Francis Hotel to be appointed radio chairman for the national and state garden clubs.

She's been orchid hunting in the Andes Mountains in Brazil, and in China where she found it necessary to defend her friend Chiang Kai-Shek, who preserved much of China's art. She was not impressed with Japan, due to their high prices, and unfortunately, China has a planting of trees along a railroad track and the Grand Canal she found to be a sewer.

Aside from her activities at Luther Burbank's at the Marin Art and Garden Center, which is in session all the time, the active octogenarian is horticulture chairman for the quarterly meetings of garden clubs from Healdsburg to Marin, held at the Luther Burbank Garden Club.

The widow of the late Dr. Tuckey, a dentist, she has one son, Robert, of Petaluma.

Born in Santa Barbara, and raised in Fresno, she had been a teacher of dental assistants at UCLA City College, where she met Dr. Tuckey.

Vignettes

Did you know that the late Paul Chirone, who has been San Anselmo's oldest pioneer, was the son of early hotel keepers? His parents' hotel was situated where the former Kaufman's men's store was located. And right near was Guasco's. How convenient for food shoppers then.

⋈

When we see hats with a flair we often think of who might wear them well. It takes a certain type to carry it off, and one such is Joan Capurro, our former Independence Savings manager, and well-known civic leader, who is a fashion plate herself. Husband Bob, an amateur artist, is a third generation San Anselman.

Do you remember little Mrs. Shutte, who came to San Anselmo as a French war bride and always walked around town with a parasol? Not a bad idea for a hot day!

⋈

The art of Percy Grey is now at a special premium, posthumously, for the San Anselmo artist died in 1950. His hillside home no doubt was the inspiration of many works.

⋈

Lucy Watson, 95-year-old town pioneer, nearly lost her home by fire as the garage and overhang were destroyed, catching fire to some of the eucalyptus trees by the home. Her daughter, Doris Pollack, was a San Anselmo bank employee whose husband is a commander of the local American Legion Post.

ooooo

Downtown San Anselmo about 1940. Alan Moder Collection.

Ferrari Stationery

How many remember Billie Ferrari? He was a young printer on the old San Anselmo Herald. If he had forgotten his lunch, my mom, the editor, would always have brought enough for Bill. Press day was too busy to luxuriate in some restaurant.

This young man was later to begin his own business, Ferrari's Stationery on San Anselmo Avenue near the present Hilda's restaurant.

His business functioned there for years. Bill and his wife lived in back of their building on Tamalpais Avenue, presently occupied by a popular restaurant.

The couple have since passed on but the firm name still exists out near the Civic Center.

Printer Kaufman

Mrs. Jack (Beth) Kaufman was another printer from the old days of the local Herald. After Beth married, she gave up her trade and became a dutiful wife and mother of two children. However, Beth wasn't one to stay home. She had lost her best friend one time in a drowning accident and decided to devote her life to teaching swimming. From conducting Red Cross classes in swimming, she became a secretary and a VIP in the International Olympics. Thousands of children were taught to swim, thereby realizing her dream.

Sea Air

San Anselmo is called inland, yet the sea gulls are frequent visitors and the sea breezes become very apparent at times. Often the warning fog horns can be heard and the sea air is so prominent we're looking for water. Not far away though, is San Francisco Bay.

During the sailing days of my late sea captain grandfather, Capt.

John O'Brien, there were no bay bridges, just easy sailing on into the San Francisco docks from Seattle or wherever. Capt. O'Brien was master on the S.S. Victoria, which command he held through the gold rush to the Yukon days. Leaving Seattle with a full load of prospective gold panners, Captain Johnny was respected for his uncanny knowledge of the icebergs in the north sea, thereby never losing a passenger or a ship.

Speaking of seafaring people, Mrs. John (Bobbie) Acree of San Rafael likes to talk of her early days at Lansdale. Her older sister was a very beautiful model at Ransohoff's in San Francisco. Bobbie would accompany her sister to the nearby train station at Lansdale where she was to board the train for the city. Little Bobbie would return home with her sister's empty coffee cup.

They were the daughters of Dr. Thomas Nelson, a ship's surgeon. Dr. Nelson was struck by a hit and run driver, incurring lifelong injuries.

Moon Walk

Our family's longtime friend Augusta Fouch, of Williams in Colusa County came across an old poem of mine written in 1968 in Long Beach called *Moon Walk*. It fits in well with this year's 20th year anniversary of the first moon walk.

> Footsteps on the moon mark man's splendor
> Imprints on time, infinite, divine
>
> Entering an age for science to render
> Proof of God's word, resounding it's heard
>
> Man stands in awe of these reverberations
> Clarions of hope widen our scope
>
> As man comprehends this magnitude of meanings
> Then nothing will defy discoveries in the sky
>
> As they pertain to earth and solve a puzzle
> As God provides a key to Eternity.

ooooo

Those Were the Days

My trip down the steep Armsby's hill in Ross on "Nellie," reinless, wasn't advisable to the more delicately raised.

It happened—all in a flash—Billie Yeo decided to take me for a horseback ride on Armsby's hill (J.K. Armsby estate is atop this considerable incline). It was paved and one of the most lateral (up and down).

Well, anyway, all went well until we reached the top when Billie threw over the reins. "Nellie" tore down at a breakneck speed, leaving my heart somewhere behind. I couldn't believe it was happening until it was over. It easily replaced all roller-coaster thrills or anything comparable.

Heckscher's Orchestra

Ernie Heckscher, he of the wonderful dance orchestra, wishes to be remembered to all his old friends.

The famed musician, raised up on Crescent Road here, a product of our schools and "Mr. Popular," in the last 50 years of dancing in Marin, is now the big rage in Palm Desert.

While at Stanford, Ernie obtained a contract with Fairmont Hotel and on the strength of that he married his childhood sweetheart, the beautiful Sally Cooley of San Anselmo. He remained with the Fairmont for 36 years, performing five nights a week.

Upon retirement, they decided to lead the "double life," seven months in Palm Desert and five months at Oakmont in Santa Rosa, all of which calls for never a dull moment.

The two have one son, Earl, also a successful bandleader and realtor. He and his wife and two daughters have lived in Atlanta, Georgia, where he performed at the Atlanta Fairmont. Their daughter Carmen has just graduated, magna cum laude, from Arizona

State University. Her sister, Marian, represents a top cosmetic firm, ScottCole Salon.

England Native

Ernie's parents, his dad from Philadelphia, and his mother, a Swiss, met in England where Ernie was born. They moved to St. Francis Woods in San Francisco when he was three years old. Early in 1920 they moved to 245 Crescent Road, San Anselmo, in a beautiful home they kept for years. Miss Valerie Ansel, local school principal for many years, occupied a cottage on their estate.

The daughter in the family, Ernie's sister, Marian succumbed to an illness in Sun City in 1987. Her husband was former General Dan Aynesworth. The couple had two sons.

Old Time Reunion

The residents of Hooper Lane, off of Lansdale Avenue here, held their second annual block party on Sunday.

Mrs. Tom Richey and Mrs. Arthur Wasserman were in charge of the hospitality committee, and all pitched in with delicious potluck offerings, cold drinks and desserts.

Weather was chilly, but soon the barbecue was going, tables set out and hearty, warm fare soon helped fill the bill. Much reminiscing was going on as former residents were honored guests. They were given tours of the houses they had grown up in and shown many new improvements. Tom Richey was showing the Beardsley brothers, Vince and Fran, the delightful changes made in their old home while Peg Richey was explaining to young people the creek bed and how it rose in the winter of '82, year of our big flood.

Movie Made

Special guest was Francis Beardsley, whose personal story was made into the movie, *Her's, Mine and Ours*, starring Lucille Ball and Henry Fonda. Fran and his wife each had children of their own, and then when they married, they had 12. They did a commercial for Langendorf Bread that supplied them with 50 loaves of bread a week, and very often an overflow was shared with those at Carmel Mission nearby their home.

A family by the name of Barnacle formerly lived in the Art Wasserman house on Hooper Lane. Three family members were there to reminisce over the old days 50 years ago when the cottages were constructed as weekend places. The Beardsley family had 12 children and the Barnacles had 13. Two full ball teams within neighboring homes. Next came the Roebury home built by an English carpenter and now occupied by Mrs. Sally Wilmington, a San Domenico employee. The latter's children are raised and she often has the convent students to her home while their parents travel. Angela with the red curls was one of these, and I told her she looked like my granddaughter, Shana.

Dancing in the Street

Tom Richey played the bass drum as his daughter, Janice McIntosh of Petaluma, rendered some personal compositions on the Scotch bagpipes and Mrs. Richey and others danced in the street. The music was good, too. Mrs McIntosh has her own band called the "McIntosh Flashers." Peg Richey, a retired school bus driver is now employed in computers for Marin Board of Education in their Corte Madera office. Their daughter is also a school bus driver in Petaluma. Arthur Wasserman is in the tax consultant business.

Out of the lives in that small corner came a hit movie telling how families managed—seeing the real people from whence it came, we found the makings of how all neighbors should live, close and caring.

Stoner's Baby

The arrival of baby Elizabeth Rose Stoner last week at Marin General Hospital added a fourth generation to the families of her parents, David and Theresa Stoner of Fairfax.

Tiny Elizabeth, named for a great-grandmother, 90-year-old Elizabeth Brandt of San Anselmo, weighed in at 9 lbs., 5 ounces.

ooooo

San Anselmo Junction at Redhill, 1940. Jack Farley Collection.

Olden But Golden

As I hark back to those days and watch my 50-year-old home movies of family and events, I can't believe the time has passed so quickly. They will be treasures for the future generations to look over some day.

Running through my mind are the fun days I had in the Ross-Kentfield area and the Ross Grammar School with its excellent staff. High in academics themselves, and ready to cope with everything, I congratulate them and their principal, Mrs. Edna Scott Lake.

Our Trains

Did you know that Marin's train system was known through the century as the most progressive and best in interurban service? Especially after 1903 when North Pacific Shore Railroad took over to make it to a broad gauge and for its electrification. It then became a "show" railroad for the U.S. for interlocking systems that kept trains from backing into one another. They employed the safety systems, semi-fors and banjo systems (including three lights).

Eugene Desablia, founder of P.G.andE. and a director of Colgate, Palmolive and Peat Co., was extremely interested in North Shore R.R. operation because of the electricity they were going to supply.

In 1872, the North Coast R.R. was established in Marin. Of course, our San Anselmo was known as the "Junction" due to the railroad arterial here. It was a center for the rail system coming from Sausalito, San Rafael and going out to Fairfax, Lagunitas and west Marin. It was a narrow gauge and received its wood out at Shafter's which had a spur two miles above Lagunitas in the middle of Paper Mill Creek. Coal was used and later steam before the electricity came in. The trains, like thread, bound the small communities together.

Longtime Residents

Robert Cary of Ross was just telling me of his family's early beginnings here and how extensive it was. His grand-uncle Dr. W.O. Jones, a general practitioner here for 50 years, had his estate right at the end of Sycamore and Madrone (now apartments). Bob's grandparents, the Clarence Symonds, held extensive property across the street (then railroad tracks) at San Anselmo Avenue and Grove Lane (later apartments) and the horse barn is still there converted into a home. A stone wall had extended around the Symonds' property. Young Bob was born there and his aunt, Edith Symonds Zastrow of Lakeport, had just phoned him and said to come and get the bed that she and later he, were born in. Her husband was Captain Curt Zastrow, commander of the Grey Lines fleet of luxury liners. He was captain of the "Santa Rosa," flagship of the fleet.

Pioneer realtor Robert Cary was Bob's father and had many sea experiences as a cabin boy and later a quartermaster. In fact he was left alone aboard a ship tied up in Oakland when the San Francisco earthquake hit in 1906. It broke the line holding to the wharf and great doings were entailed to return it. He later was with Matson Line and made a trip around the Horn with the second S.S. Lurline. In 1910 he came to San Anselmo at the suggestion of a brother in law, Fred Crocker who had been married to Alice Symonds, Bob's aunt.

Bob who lives with his wife, Virginia, in Ross, is a very amenable person and to do him justice we are to conclude this story in the later edition.

Info on a Local Teacher

James McDearmon, of Turlock, is a retired professor in linguistics and speech from Stanislaus State University, was raised here in San Anselmo, and is very enthusiastic about San Anselmo history. His wife, Kay, is an author of many children's books and the two had this column mailed to them by her sister, Lillian Gassner of San Anselmo.

He sent us a letter explaining what kind of teacher Miss Valerie Ansel was. The local principal, always controversial, succumbed in a Grass Valley nursing home this past year while in her 90s.

German Delicatessens

Virginia Baxus of Mill Valley was a member of San Anselmo's Vonderheide family. This included two major German delicatessen owners within a mile. One downtown next to the current liquor store was owned and run by Fred and Henrietta Kappelman. She was the sister of Elizabeth Vonderheide, who with her husband, Fred, operated a similar store in Lansdale. The latter couple had three children, Henry, a Fairfax policeman; August, a San Francisco commercial printer; and a daughter, Mrs. Anna Blackford of San Anselmo.

Virginia was the daughter of August Vonderheide and was raised across the Bay but later joined her widowed mother here. The latter was for many years a bookkeeper for the Lucas Valley Dairy run by the Grady family in San Rafael.

Reminiscing of her commutes to San Francisco, Mrs. Baxus said, "Bumper to bumper over the Corte Madera grade to the city was no joke either! At least 101 is even." Her two brothers-in-law were famed baseball players. Jim Baxus was a third baseman for the Cleveland Indians and Hollywood Stars and brother, Mike Baxus, was playing first base for the San Francisco Seals.

She was a niece of the late Arthur and Clara Shearer, San Anselmo pioneers, and a cousin of the late Helen Shearer Jenkinson of Murray Park.

Mrs. Vonderheide and Mrs. Shearer were close sisters and lived to be 94 and 96, respectively. They died within a year of one another.

Parade Comments

Parade Day in San Anselmo recently was exciting, timed well and the best show was all the kids in and out of the parade. The streets were packed with preschoolers. Is this a baby boom year? We'd better look to our schools. Buying them back won't be easy. Yes, the elderly were there too, some sweet old couples proudly walking along, many grey-haired proud of their town. "Noah's Ark" packed with tiny tots had "Noah" himself there. One gentleman ran over with his baby and handed him over to a mother in The Ark. The kids were joyous when candy was thrown to them. Some enterprising little girls were selling lemonade in front of a restaurant.

The Marines led off in white uniforms and a roar of applause greeted them. The fire trucks and their sirens, boys doing bicycle tricks, crack horse riders so straight on their mounts, with braided manes and tails and ribbons. Music bands playing on trucks, dancing girls and their twirling batons all marched past the reviewing stands positioned on Tunstead by Wells Fargo Bank.

Missing Link

The phone rang and it was son Harry in Bangor, Maine. I had asked him if he could look for an old family graveyard of Samuel Smith and wife, Rachel. The man was my great-great grandfather and related to the Hinckleys and Austins of the area. Report from Harry was that four more graveyards were to be investigated but if no success, the only place would have been the St. John River. Samuel Smith ... where are you?

Relativity

"We were at Plymouth Rock"
My uncle had told me
Some mysteries to unlock
Or just for identity

"You're a Smith," Auntie said
You have all the traits."
Ignoring my red head
And turning the fates.

My cousin said, never forget
The Pacific Northwest's
Instilled in you yet.
Your ancestor rests.

But then Bangor, Maine
Keeps cropping up
I needn't be sane
Just a little mixed up.

—Larine Brown 6/1/89

ooooo

Memories Linger

Memories linger ... this ol' town has been through many a catastrophe—flood, fire, earthquake and war in addition to depression, but still keeps rolling along.

The determined pioneer spirit still prevails regardless of the new life-styles. The lovely tree-lined streets, now in fall colors, are well preserved. Many cottages built for those leaving San Francisco in the 1906 earthquake are standing, renovated, but the same structures. This population segment hangs on to prideful roots and promotes the better qualities in their children.

Keeping up with the Joneses

Bob Cary's family story began last week, entailing six generations, including a great-grandfather, Thomas Jones, who arrived in San Francisco in 1844. Jones left to continue studies at Cambridge, returning in 1849. His bride, the daughter of an English army officer stationed in Australia, had originally come to the City to marry Jones' best friend, who died before she arrived. She fell in love with Tom during her visit and the two were married.

Jones Crossing

Dr. Ottiwell Wood Jones, longtime practicing physician here, lived in a large home at the end of Sycamore and Madrone streets, and across the railroad tracks (now Center Boulevard) resided his sister, husband and family on Grove Lane and San Anselmo Avenue. They were Clarence Symonds, wife Martha Ann and family. He was an executive with the American Can Company. This crossing was later and still is called the Jones Crossing. Dr. Jones was a grand-uncle of Bob Cary and Mrs. Symonds was Bob's grandmother. The Symonds family finally left San Anselmo, selling here and buying a large area of Chicken Point, now Bayside Acres.

Other brothers were Will Jones, who lives on Laurel Avenue and worked for Shreve and Co.; Hubert, who owned a place at Lagunitas, and young Tom of San Francisco. The son of the doctor, Dr. O.W. Jones, Jr., a neurosurgeon of Sleepy Hollow, recently succumbed. He practiced with Dr. Naffziger, San Francisco dean of brain surgery.

The Bob Carys have two sons, Dr. R. Todd Cary, San Rafael, dentist, and Keith Cary, a plant pathologist married with one daughter. Todd is a member of the San Anselmo Rotary Club, married to the former Heidi Hickingbotham, a descendant of Captain Robert Dollar of San Rafael. The couple have five children, the eldest of whom, Kimberly, a graduate of Georgetown University, is now on the staff of Vogue Magazine.

⊷⊶

"We're going to sell until the shelves are clean," says Kenneth Harris, co-owner of Rossi Bros. Pharmacy in San Anselmo, the historic drugstore which is going out of business this month after 60 years.

Hundreds of old-time customers are paying their last respects, as it were, to the store, its clerks and pharmacists, and pining for the old store, a leading local landmark.

The Rossi brothers, Frank and Joseph, opened in their own building back in the '30's. The rear inside wall was adorned by a painting by the late Jose Moya Del Pino, world renowned artist. Joseph Rossi still lives in Ross and Frank Rossi's widow lives in Kentfield.

Mr. Harris, who with Charles Locati owns this pharmacy and Lockwood's in Mill Valley, said the sale is for economic reasons. Competition from discount drugstores and rent raising is forcing their hand. Mill Valley will soon have a Long's store. The local store was in the present hands for 28 years since the Rossi brothers retired. Clerk Selena Graham of San Rafael, and pharmacist Hugh Houston have been with the firms all that time. Al Andrade, a pharmacist, has worked for them 12 years and Betty Kettman, a clerk, for five years.

The prescription file will go to the local Jack's Drug Store as will some of the employees. This is the third family business folding here in recent years, preceded by Kaufman's Department Store and Kientz's Bakery.

Old Timer Reminiscences

James McDearmon, a retired English professor in Turlock, who was raised in San Anselmo, communicates about the Heckscher family that appeared last week. Re. Ernie he states, "I knew Ernie Heckscher and his sister Marian. We were in public speaking class together and she was very nice. Bob taught Ernie to drive. When he was younger he had a home movie—*The Lost World* about dinosaurs and I went with my brothers Bob and Fielding. The movie was in their garage on a very large estate. I walked by it often to see a friend Jack Bergner, a very talented artist. He drew in the class when the teacher was talking. Where is Jack now?"

Cement Lost

Did you know that 5,000 sacks of cement were lost in the flood of 1926 by the Home Market here? The former grocery and meat market owned by the late Gabriel Franchini across from Wells Fargo Bank was situated in such a place as to bear the brunt of floods. It was another local business that was sold and is now occupied by a series of shops in an arcade and a restaurant. Bill Franchini, my informant, has promised more on his family.

ooooo

San Anselmo in 1900. From left to right: Red Hill; Old Captain Foss House (with cupola), later Baner House superseded by First Presbyterian Church; Crisp House; (in foreground) two barns for Bouicks' and Days' horses and cows; (on knoll) San Francisco Theological seminary; Alex Bouick house; Minton house (later Wicher, Oxtoby, etc.); stable; (far right) Mackenzie house (later MacIntosh, Admin Bldg, etc.); stable; Alexander house (later Paterson, Krueger etc.); Day House (later Oxtaby, Sr., Donald Stewart, etc., till demolished about 1956); lastly Montgomery Chapel. Roy Farrington Jones Private Library.

Remember When...

I'm almost a native Californian, came in from Seattle as a tot, and even as I write the earth is moving. Grandma was a native though, and loved her state. Emily O'Brien was born and raised in San Diego.

My eyes are glued to Channel 7 ... communicators are feeling this aftershock too. So I'll see how they react as I'm not sure whether to get under the doorway as I did last week.

Shades of other quake moments: while living in Long Beach in the 1971 quake, our bed rolled all around the floor at 6 a.m.; the quake series we had in the early '80's, when my cat literally clung to me; and now I'm still shaken from the Oct. 17, 1989 earthquake. San Anselmo was moved around a bit in 1957 too.

In my last column I spoke of earthquakes, fires, etc. and how the spirit of man continues on with courage. A week later we had the chance to prove it. My column turned prophetic when I thought it would be passé with so much baseball series talk. However, I was right on.

Seminary Hill

San Anselmo has a great center for Christian education in the San Anselmo Presbyterian Theological Seminary on Kensington and Austin Streets. Its campus makes a lovely tour for visitors with its great trees, similar to those in Palestine. Over 30 buildings and homes stand in, on and around the old-world woods and pastures of Seminary Hill, looking over Ross Valley to Mt. Tamalpais.

Its founder was William Anderson Scott, prophet, preacher and scholar. Since he had arrived in San Francisco in 1854 he resolved that he would start the Presbyterian Seminary within sight of the Bay. Within 17 years his dream became reality when in 1871 the

Synod of the Pacific elected a Board of Directors with orders to "organize a theological seminary such as present want and future interests of this coast demands." It was begun in November with four professors and four students.

First lodgings were in the back of Old St. John's Presbyterian Church, where Dr. Scott was pastor. Move to the present campus was in September, 1889 when Arthur W. Foster, trustee and son-in-law of Dr. Scott donated the 21-acre site overlooking this valley. Following a $250,000 gift from pioneer merchant Alexander Montgomery, construction was begun for the new buildings. Dedication in an all-day ceremony was September 21, 1892. One newspaper called the new Seminary in San Anselmo, with its magnificent stone castles, "the rising star of the west."

Today as one of 11 seminaries of the Presbyterian Church (U.S.A.) with students from over 30 denominations it is committed to education for faithful Christian witness. Currently, there are 23 full time professors and instructors, six visiting lecturers and 86 adjunct professors. They are all of high credential from the world's finest universities. A thousand students are enrolled in degree programs and 3,000 in non-degree conference and seminars.

Life of Jewells

There they were ... George and Inez Jewell a couple that has grown with San Anselmo. Inez, having been a Massara, is an excellent cook and served a delightful lunch. She was a young girl raised in Ross who had married a young fellow in the army air corps, George Jewell. He joined the San Anselmo Fire Department in June of 1951 when it only had ten paid men and retired in February of 1976 just short of his 54th birthday. During World War II he had been a radio operator in the air corps serving in India, Burma and China.

George now belongs to a number of civic and church groups and is a golfer. The couple keeps active and enjoy their daughter, Sandy, who lives nearby and son, Gary of Petaluma, who works for the city of Novato. Their pets include a little 10-year-old dog named Coco and a new puppy rescued from a family of neglected animals in Santa Cruz.

Clippings

Scrapbooks describe the life of an active fireman; picturing George holding a hose, walking gingerly over burned boards; assisting a dazed Fire Chief Richard McLaren after a ceiling fell on him; rescuing a youth from drowning in the creek at Samuel Taylor Park; paying honors to Capt. Robert Meagor, whose death in the '30's was the only one of the local department and planting a memorial garden honoring the late Judge Fred Crisp.

Inez was always an active wife and mother in church and school activities, often seen bringing a hot meal over to George at the fire house. She held a regular office job retiring after many years service. They love their comfortable home located near the town center.

Like all towns or cities in America, San Anselmo is known for its bona fide Christian worship centers of all denominations. Finding a church "home" is all important where a believer can feel comfortable and at ease in the congregation. Christian churches are based on the teachings of Jesus Christ and the Bible with appropriate sermons. Today God's word is penetrating life-styles as never before but man proposes and God disposes.

The Bear

The famous piece of sculpture, the Bear, done by the famed Benjamino Buffano in 1965, and located in front of the Ross Police Department, has just undergone repair. Some cracks in the marble composite were refinished by the Buffano Society of Mill Valley. It is a typical piece done by the artist at the height of his career. Donation was made to the town in 1971 by Mr. and Mrs. Jerome Flax of Ross.

Chris Monte

The Charles Montes are proud of their daughter, Christine Monte, who is rally commissioner for Marin Catholic High School. Also on the cross country running team, she is an avid runner.

Their son, Steve, is an exchange student in Madrid and son, Matthew, is attending the University of Hawaii.

On Earthquakes
My mind had risen
Like a Richter Scale
Emotions imprisoned
Like a submerged gale.

The rain was coming
Down on campers' tents
And gullies were running
Where the earth was rent.

While spirits had dampened
The new crews came in
And hope ran rampant
As they stood to win.

—Larine Brown
10-26-89

ooooo

Sweet Bye and Bye. . .

Mother earth went crazy in the tremor that took off like a belly dancer last October 17 and people are still talking. When the very ground under your feet can't be depended on, what can? Terra firma was no longer that.

San Anselmans came through in aiding the quake victims. Robert Mitchell of the Easy Street Cafe in the Red Hill Shopping Center was so pleased that the life of his brother, Chris, was spared that he organized a caravan of food dispensers to the rescuers at the 880 bridge disaster. Chris climbed out of his Escort wagon when it was buried under the upper deck of the freeway. Checks have been pouring into Salvation Army and Red Cross disaster relief.

Out-of-state relatives have panicked about their loved ones after watching the TV accounts of the crushing loss in the Bay Area and Santa Cruz. Marin, however, remained safe, but the chimney people were booked solid. Bricks can be loosened and fall easily.

Charlie Brown

My late husband, Charles, was senior inspector for the State Division of Architecture. His inspections included many of the areas that were hardest hit in the quake. Charlie was born on October 21, 1906 the year of the first big quake and succumbed May 16, 1989, the year of the next big one, which landed five days before his birthday. He was very knowledgeable in construction and was spared an inspector's nightmare of cracking rebar and faulty construction. Although retired, his interest still lay in the buildings of the state.

Larry Wright

We found Larry Wright, popular local attorney, last week all decked out (his office was) in birthday attire. He had been celebrating one of the big "0's" and was reminiscing, with legal talk, of early San Anselmo. He and his wife Elizabeth moved into the Winship Park tract and his office opened on April 1, 1948 in the old building owned by Frances Dudley Mayall (now housing the liquor store). In 1952 A. Von Rotz cleared off some acacia trees a block away and constructed office buildings, one of which Wright has occupied ever since.

He was a native of Des Moines, Iowa, and graduated from Duke University in Durham, North Carolina. The couple has four children, Jim, Gary, Charles and Libby, all of whom live out of the county.

Ruth Whiting, Wright's office secretary and crew had engineered some clever office decorating, one of which expressed sentiments in words with candy bars—"You are such a BIG HUNK that we would climb the highest MOUNTAIN, go to FIFTH AVENUE or even MARS or the MILKY WAY to see you. You look great U*No and we wanted to give you a CUP O' GOLD or at least a CHUCKLES because you are the best BAR NONE." So the placard said and we agree.

Homecoming Queen

Christine Monte was elected Homecoming Queen at Marin Catholic High School Saturday night after the game. At the dance that followed, her dad, Charles Monte, and fathers of the nine princesses had the first dance with their daughters. Chrissy is a blonde edition of her father, who is owner of Chapel of the Hills. They are grandchildren of San Anselmo pioneers the late Harry and Katy Brown.

During the school ceremonies Saturday a memorial to Donald Ongaro, the late owner of Ongaro's Plumbing, was conducted. He was killed in a road accident earlier this year, saddening the many friends he had here.

Stagecoach

To celebrate the 80th anniversary of the Wells Fargo Bank, the local branch has a half-size replica of the original stagecoach on display.

The red and yellow coach was an attraction in Buffalo Bill Cody's

Wild West Show. Cody rode the coach at full speed into the arena, firing his Colt revolvers all the way. He rode pony express at 14 and later was a buffalo hunter, army scout, plainsman and showman.

The coach of special interest to children is nine feet, seven inches long and seven feet, six inches high, red and yellow, bought from James Draper of Boston.

Paul Chirone

Paul Chirone, San Anselmo, pioneer, has been presented with a certificate of appreciation by the San Anselmo Post No. 179, Department of California American Legion.

According to Herman Woods, Commander and Donald B. Gold, chairman coordinator, Chirone has contributed to the advancement of the Legion programs and activities dedicated to God and country.

Deaths

The last week brought two deaths of local well-known men, Art Smith, former mayor of the town and Merrill Williamsen, longtime employee of the local post office. Both left widows, children and grandchildren.

ooooo

Seminary about 1900. May-Murdock Publications.

Yesterday ... Yesterday

Sitting alone with my friend, trying to mentally digest the quake and post-quake activities as we run along into holiday fare. An added air of togetherness with exciting stories to tell is prevailing. My friend realizes I'm getting preoccupied and ceases as an attention getter, settling down to a comfortable purr. She's been with me since I began the column. Let me introduce "Missy," a young female of mixed origin. Resembling the Siamese, she's a throwback from a family of stripers. Oddly enough, she resembles my 17-year-old disgruntled Siamese (mixed), Mai Tai. The latter, highly resentful, carried on badly with hissing, spitting hostility (this was a my-house-first type of thing). Missy holds her own and they are accepting now. So be it. Cats! ! Great predictors for earthquakes, though.

The old holidays we used to have in Marin when our kids were growing up are so nice to look back on—the small communities of Fairfax, San Anselmo, Ross and Kentfield, in which people intermingled. And most knew one another, if they weren't related or lived in the same neighborhood. Mothers mostly stayed home in those days and managed creative outlets from there. When mothers were forced into the work market, a neighbor, if not an older relative, was usually available for the children.

Seminary Trees

An arboretum for all to see was created on the grounds of the San Francisco Theological Seminary over the years by trustees, architects and groundskeepers.

A 90-minute stroll through the grounds with a map and guide book could enrich your average sightseer.

In front of Montgomery Hall stands Bouick Oak, the California white oak planted in 1885 as part of a typical open chaparral landscape. At the crest of the hill by Geneva Hall are a stand of valley and black oak. Bouick Oak is named in honor of Alexander Bouick, superintendent of the building and grounds during the Seminary's first 30 years at its San Anselmo location. When he died in 1922, the graduating class donated funds for a stone wall and concrete bench and most of the walk down the hill. Students loved Bouick as he listened to their sermons candidly with a kindly criticism. Nearby stands the smaller black oak that has pointed, not rounded, leaves.

Old Corner

Jack Minnes, original owner of Jack's Drug Store had a brother who was a look alike to Bob Taylor, widow's peak and all. The store was situated where the present Patrick Brothers is now. Hungry for movie idols, many women would drive slowly by to get a look at the younger brother in the prescription department. In earlier years the corner had a drugstore run by Mrs. Shapiro with the black hair in a bun, who made her own tooth powder and was often counted on for medical advice when doctor wasn't available.

Jimmie Flynn

Congratulations to Jimmie Dee Flynn of Fairfax in her "Celebration of Life" program she conducted last week at Church of the Nazarene. Jimmie is an unbelievably active person for one in a wheelchair and was giving thanks to God for overcoming her recent illness. Various friends gave encouraging talks, her background was discussed and her family introduced including her mother, Mrs. Doris Flynn of San Anselmo, a constant worker for all the handicapped. Her brother-in-law, Rev. William Eudy and wife, Kelli, Jimmie's sister, as well as young 13-year-old Nancie, were there. The Eudy's three children Amy, April and Andrew were also present. The Eudys live in Willits where he has been designated as the new minister to the church there.

Music of the "Soul Singers" proved a captivating conclusion.

ooooo

American Party

Americans are party people ... and the great American Christ-mas party is now in full swing. At every turn we are reminded that Santa Claus is on his way ... and how! The street decor is abundant, the stores pleasing customers and the great "buy" is on. The cheer and joy is retained in this country and the happiness of gift exchanges and parties make it an exciting time.

This year the population density is being felt more, and gridlock continues at an alarming pace (hope the insurance companies follow through on the new ideas for gauging accidents including density). But through it all, as in Bay Areans in the Quake of October, the American spirit is indomitable. Maybe they would return the train service back to us. It's a great way for massive transit.

Lost Weekend

We left Centerville, Utah the Saturday after Thanksgiving with happy enough thoughts. Then about 4 p.m. between Boomtown and Truckee we (five of us in a new Pontiac) encountered one of the worst snow and rain blizzards of all time (the Donners had nothing on us), on top of that there was "gridlock" for many miles. For four hours we inched along. Everyone in the area but the weary travelers knew about the storm and the gridlock. We spent some hours sleeping in the car and our driver doesn't want to see snow again, thank you. After resting up in San Anselmo, away they went home to Willits. They know Donner Pass!

Our delightful hosts, Hal and Fran Cheney, had returned to and artfully redecorated their old homestead, which had been occupied by prior generations, in Utah. They had raised a family of four in Walnut Creek where he taught English and was liaison officer for the local schools.

Utah to San Anselmo

Somewhere between Truckee and Boomtown
Traffic had stopped with a lock

The gridlock began further on down
It was from 4 until 10 o'clock.

We ran out of what to say
And questioned a thousand times

We then started to pray
In a lengthening of the lines.

We turned around, driving back
Spirits sodden and down.

New driven snow, as a fact
Had driven us back into town.

No room at the inn they said
We felt like Joseph and Mary.

Inquiring from many, we pled
Ash, Em, Lilly and Harry.

We slept in the car that night.
It wasn't what we wanted.

But we had gridlock fright
And preferred to stay undaunted.

Minute by minute reports on the radio
Said the same old thing.

No chains were a "no-no"
The Cal-Trans ring-a-ding.

Sun was bright on the new fallen snow
A fairy land was beholden.

Weary travelers still didn't know
What direction they were sold on.

Facing lines with no progress
Or back to no room at the inn.

We finally did digress
Softening our chagrin.

Icicles formed on the windows passed
A third time the traffic was free

Weary bones had us outclassed
Just five of us, family and me.

—Larine Brown
11/26/89

Forty Years Ago

Children in San Anselmo had Santa Claus to talk to down at the city hall lawn where his workshop was, as well as the manger scene, for which the local firemen were responsible. The jolly ol' gent himself, Santa Claus, was played by Dan McCarthy of Mack's Photo. He interviewed the little ones and there were pictures for their mothers to collect. Somehow my youngest was getting it all together in his mind in associating the babe in the manger and Jesus the carpenter. Finally, he said, "Mom, let's go back and see the dead carpenter."

Our late brother-in-law, D. Frank Monte, former mayor of the town and impresario extraordinaire, did a bang-up job as Santa due to his natural ho-ho and understanding way with kids. He was multi-talented, often sang, did comic bits for the service clubs' plays and was director of war bond sales at the local theatre. Dr. Kenneth Galbraith, local podiatrist, a distinguished white-haired gentleman anyway, was often placed appropriately in the role by family and friends in his neighborhood. Our nephew, big Buzz Brown of Yolanda, was often a perfect match for the part with his jolly attitude, which to date is still existing. Ho-Ho, Buzz!

The Missing Link

As I pulled into my driveway the other night I found that Toyota truck there that had belonged to my late husband. I had given it to son Dave, after his was crashed, and when I entered my home, it was son Harry, from Willits, who had traded vehicles temporarily as Dave needed a 4-wheel drive up at Mt. Shasta. So Harry was standing there. He was on the phone talking to our newfound cousin, Nick Roth, of Larkspur. Thereby hangs the tale. Nick read my story about Harry searching the Bangor, Maine archives for great-grandfather Samuel Smith. It seems Nick is also related to the Smiths, Austins, and Miles Standish of Plymouth Rock fame. So what does that make me? A descendent of Standish? Anyway, my Smiths that landed in Seattle in 1838 kept good records but this was our missing link! Nick is to mail me his genealogy so I can hardly wait. Our family has one but doesn't mention the late Mr. Standish.

A timely story of folks who conducted the first Thanksgiving, eating the available food and thanking God for saving their lives on the crude rock-bound coast of the New World.

Get well wishes are many for Frances Moder, San Anselmo resident for 40 years, who underwent surgery last week in a local hospital. She and her late husband Marty are parents of four sons, one of whom, Alan, resides with her at their local home.

⊶⊷

At this reading I will have enplaned to Atlanta, Georgia, the star city of the east, to spend Christmas with daughter, son-in-law, and grandchildren Pat, John, Ron, Ric, John and Shana. They live in the suburb of Dunwoody. The southern hospitality is real, as well as the grits, and the family life that's a part of it.

See you in 1990! Merry Christmas and Happy New Year.

ooooo

Atlanta—Star City

I landed Wednesday from Atlanta so I haven't really found my ground legs yet. How do world travelers do it anyway? I spent nearly four hours seated on a plane, except for the tippy walking to the r.r.—rough weather enters invariably at that moment.

Atlantans nearly assaulted me, with questions about the S.F. quake and I explained that we, in Marin, heard the same TV reports they did, except for the fact that we felt the tremendous ground upheaval. Many were commuters, or had family and friends there and were closer to the scene so picked up the anxiety by osmosis, I explained.

Anyway, I thoroughly enjoyed the big "C" in Atlanta with our offspring there and had the true southern welcome. The family, nine of us, none true Atlantans, except for its head, John, had one of the happiest times ever; with one Canadian, one Nebraskan, five ex-Bay Areans, one southerner and me, the San Anselman.

Arctic weather dogged us with zero temps, unheard of in the South, and snow fell lightly at Christmas. The star city of the South is extremely progressive with natural woods being cleared for more buildings like in Marin, in a gigantic way. One conservative was bold enough to say in the paper we'd better replace our bumper stickers with "Save the Planet."

⋈

More notes came in from Jim McDearmon, the linguistics professor from Stanislaus University who was raised in San Anselmo. He wanted to remind us of the great "ambergris" hunt at Stinson Beach in 1934. Many thought it would be lucrative but it turned out to be pollution, i.e., sewage. Then there was Jack Beckett, another San Anselmo youth, who attended San Anselmo Main School. He later became president and board chairman of Transamerica for an extended period. His picture was in full page ads for the company in *Time* and *Newsweek*. The Pyramid was built when he ran the company. A note about the famed athlete Sam Chapman, a high school chum of many, who made All American for football and baseball and is now listed in the Hall of Fame at Canton, Ohio. At Tamalpais High he was a competitor in an intramural boxing show—one night with a brawny friend. Neither wanted to hurt the other, so they danced about gingerly nearly putting the audience to sleep. Sam is married and lives in Marin.

Another was the clever young artist Howard Brodie, whose career was budding at Tam High where he entertained readers with sketches of the teachers and student body. Jim said he studied at California School of Fine Arts, worked at Huntington Library and was on the sport staff of the *San Francisco Chronicle*. He was also listed in *Who Was Who in American Art* for 1985. He was born November 28, 1916.

Tam High Teachers

Jim has mentioned three teachers at Tamalpais High School he believed were as good as any at college and I agree. One was Ruby Scott, who could "rattle off her Latin more fluently than most people speak English." My note is that she was the best Latin teacher in the state. She commuted daily on the ferries from her home in Oakland where she resided with a widowed mother. Dr. Albertine Nash, Jim said, was the only Ph.D. on a high school faculty that he had ever known and was a positively brilliant person and speaker.

Last but not least to be mentioned was Francis B. Waterman, highly popular English and journalism teacher. He related to youth and knew how to motivate them. They gladly did their work for him.

These teachers were mostly active in the '20's, '30's and '40's.

Eve Arden

Of course, we must add the very clever actress Eve Arden, who as Eunice Quedens of Mill Valley was a star of the Tam High productions. Her budding high school years on stage were fraught with incidents that any actress would find distracting to her performance.

Her slip fell in the middle of a serious drama (strap broke) and she picked it up and went on. A tale from some of her school co-players was when the prop glass was missing, she held her hand out for a glass of lemonade and her co-player, not noting the absence of her glass, poured the liquid all over her gown. She laughed it off with the audience. What else could she do?

ooooo

Old Ford Tin Lizzie about 1900 in Ross with the Rattrey family. May–Mur-dock Publications.

Our Good Neighbors

I thought the rains would never come with forecasters biting their nails when we heard the low soft sound on an early Friday morning. My skylights were going pitter-patter through the glass. Heaven had loosed its blessings. Hallelujah! Rain again. I cherish the down spouts, and those roaring gutters that you hope have no leaves.

There are several situations involving heritage and the geriatric set that I just have to get off my chest.

Praise to those who go beyond duties' call to help the aged in nursing homes, so often understaffed. For years, Helen Pederson of Woodacre has contributed a bright touch with her bedside flowers, artistic displays and entertainment. It's real to the elderly and touches them where they are. Artie Hecht, former local butcher, has been a cheery bright spot for them. Betty Muirhead of San Rafael is a hard working volunteer who began when her mother was ill and continued on at Fifth Avenue Convalescent even after her mother's demise. The Redwoods Retirement Home Auxiliary in Greenbrae honored Dorothy Chamberlin of Mill Valley at a special dinner. Dorothy has been tireless in her aid to the helpless and aged.

Cameo of Yesterday

Scene from the past: It was about 1930 and the neighborhood boys got together over the perennial car, auto or Tin Lizzie. Four heads bent over a Model T in the Stoner's backyard; namely Ed and Bob Stoner, Charlie and Ed Brown. Charlie, the natural mechanic, said it was the only car he's seen run in reverse. You'd have to be one to know the meaning.

Indian Logo

Powers that be at Tamalpais High School. It's hard to draw ethnic lines after many generations of high school students were proud to have the "Indian" banner. What's more Indian than "Tamalpais" or the mountain by that name under which it stands. The sleeping maiden atop was like a silent guardian and the American natives' heritage became our own. By changing our old alma mater's insignia there could be ethnic problems. We felt a loving kindness to the Indian, our peace loving natives that preceded us.

Howard Brodie

There were few in Marin that hadn't heard of Howard Brodie and today he is remembered. The prolific artist that pleased the Tamalpais High student body of then and now. The name means the magic of a wonderful creative gift that soared him to fame of his day; *Life*, *Colliers*, *S.F. Chronicle* and "The Yank" of army distinction.

Brodie is the son of Howard and Anna Brodie of Oakland. His attendance at the Mill Valley high school brought his talent to the eye of locals and he gained much adulation. He went on as an art journalist to cover every major sports event, several wars and many major court trials, i.e., the Manson trial. His sketches told their own tales.

Long residents of Palo Alto, he and his wife Isabel moved to Carmel to reside in a five-acre wooded area atop Jack's Peak. They were joined by their daughter, Wendy, a professional chef and her husband Alan Altrac. Their compound includes studios for both Brodie and Isabel, who do collages! He has seen four wars, five executions, seven major criminal trials and is an opponent to the death penalty. He is a teacher at the Academy of the Arts in San Francisco and plans to create until he dies.

First Baptist Church, San Anselmo

Reverend Paul Keeler sent us this recount of the First Baptist Church's local history:

"Sixty-one years ago this past July, the First Baptist Church of San Anselmo was begun by a chance meeting between a salesman and customer in her home. Discovering they were both Baptists, the salesman, Rev. Arthur Collins and the customer, Mrs. J.G. Vickery made plans for weekly worship services.

"They recruited seven others and on July 15, 1928, the group signed a document establishing the Marin County Baptist Church. For a time the group used the San Anselmo Women's Improvement Club on Tunstead Avenue in San Anselmo. As attendance at the services grew, they were forced to look for a larger building in which to meet.

"With the help of the American Baptist Home Mission Society, the membership secured a temporary meeting place. In January 1930, the railroad Chapel Car, "Good Will" was moved into a railroad siding near the hub (junction of Sir Francis Drake and Redhill Avenue). The chapel car beautifully served the church's needs for the next year.

"At the end of that period the congregation was able to purchase ground for a building at the corner of Sir Francis Drake and Sais in San Anselmo. A small building was dedicated on this corner on December 7, 1930.

"In April, 1942, the name of the church was changed to its present name, The First Baptist Church of San Anselmo.

"Dedication of the present church building at 921 Sir Francis Drake took place in January 1953. A Sunday School and Social Hall was added in the summer of 1962.

"I assumed my pastoral duties at First Baptist Church in May, 1974 and became the 24th pastor in the 61 year history of the church.

"The church presently gathers for worship on Sunday mornings at 11:00 a.m. Sunday School is at 9:45 and Bible study and prayer meeting at 7:00 on Wednesday evenings."

ooooo

Sleepy Hollow Ranch in San Anselmo with 240 cows. Alan Moder Collection.

February!

Spring showers bring May flowers. You say, "What a learned statement. Did college help in that respect?" Maybe not, but it does tell the Marin weather story and why it is more attractive to the affluent for year round weather. Just barely February and we are in spring weather. Anyway, hearts and flowers time, planting and pruning is keeping the gardeners busy. I prefer my flowers already blooming. There are so many fatalities in my plant row. Overflooding, leaving in drafts or by the fire following an overnight freeze just isn't conducive to good health. Common sense would say no. I am now considering the artificial for something green.

The Stoner Family

We never know ahead where we'll find a wealth of family history. We discovered the Stoner families came in here around 1915 from San Jose and Cleveland, Ohio. Two brothers left Southampton and Brighton-on-the-Sea, England, where their father was a boat captain, for Cleveland where they met two attractive sisters and married them. George Stoner was wed to Mary Frances Painter, while Henry took her sister, Jane, as his bride. They first worked at Agnes State Hospital at San Jose, moving into the Ross Valley in 1915 to reside and raise their children.

George bought two lots in the current Sleepy Hollow on Butterfield Road across from the Cunha Dairy, later turned into a riding academy. This was located near the present fire house out there. Their first home had three sides covered by porch, customary in that day. That house is still standing but remodeled. George became the sexton at St. John's Episcopal Church in Ross, and he became a citizen on September 7, 1915. To find work in the munitions plant in Cleveland, the family moved there—that is Mary Frances, Charles and Robert while Edward was born there on February 1, 1918. They then purchased the home on Elm Avenue from Gus Adams in 1925 for the sum of $10. There was a three-room shack, but as the family grew it was improved and expanded to 12 rooms. Charles Stoner died on August 19, 1925 of acute appendicitis. George passed on in 1944 and his wife in 1970.

Son Robert Stoner lives in El Cerrito with wife, Joyce. They have two children and grandchildren. He is a Southern Pacific accountant retiree.

Edward and his wife, Vanda, have three children and three grandchildren, and they reside in San Anselmo. He belongs to the SIRS (Sons in Retirement) and was a computer programmer for Southern Pacific before retiring.

Clare Stoner lives in the family home on Elm Avenue. She retired from Chevron Corporation and belongs to several Chevron retirement groups and is an officer in the Marin Solos, a Senior dance group.

Ida May (Stoner) Colins resides in Novato and has five children and 11 grandchildren.

George's brother, Henry and wife resided in Fairfax where they raised a son, Howard, who later became manager of stores in Sacramento, Walnut Creek and Sonora, where Howard and wife now live. Their son, Henry and wife Jane moved up to the area that's now Rohnert Park and ran a compound of cabins, gas station and cafeteria, later moving to the Burchart Apts. in San Rafael.

Paul Chirone

Old San Anselmans will miss Paul Chirone whose death occurred this week at Marin General Hospital. Paul was born here where his folks had a hotel (located where Kaufman's men's store was). His business had been landscape gardening and as a friend he was constantly giving to others, especially the needy. Paul was a war veteran, recently honored by the American Legion post, and earlier a skilled runner taking the lead in many a Dipsea race at Stinson Beach.

ooooo

San Anselmo Focus

I was just musing about the old days, 1921, when my Seattle family moved into Kentfield for my father's health. Ned O'Brien, fatally ill after a sea accident, succumbed a year later. The vine-covered cottage with porches, where we lived on Kent Avenue, was named "Reilly Wild," for its owner, James Reilly, San Francisco mortician. Reilly was a friend of Ned's father, Captain John A. O'Brien, whose 60 years at sea were captured in his biography. My mother, Agnes, went to the San Anselmo Herald to be hired as reporter and editor.

Byron D. Box was then the publisher. His son, Davis, married the daughter of Dr. Clark of Ross General Hospital. Often the Box family would take us on camping trips to the northern rivers.

The old Herald offices were located on Tunstead Avenue, next to Shearer's plumbing and across the street from the current Jack's Drug Store. One of the printers was Beth Kaufman, whose print work ended when she married Jack Kaufman and had two children. She later became a secretary for the swimming division of the Olympics. Her good friend had drowned and she devoted much time to teaching Marin's children to swim. Beth said for years the walls of the old Herald office held the printers' hieroglyphics. The early Herald press is now in possession of the San Anselmo Historical Museum located in the San Anselmo Library basement.

Back to the family: Mrs. Edna Scott Lake, principal of Ross Grammar School, welcomed the three of us as my grandma, Emily O'Brien, brought us in for registration that first fall. She said, "You live barely over the line in Kentfield, but I want to keep those lovely children with me." My sister, Pat, a beauty, had long auburn curls; brother John, a handsome brown-haired lad, and I had light red hair. We stayed on here as grandma, a native of San Diego, had given her heart to San Francisco. She would await the arrival of Captain O'Brien's ship, the S.S. Victoria, coming through the Golden Gate for S.F., thence to Nome, Alaska.

Oldies but Goodies

America's jazz bands of the '40s, playing background music for many of today's seniors, are sweeping the country. Dominican's Angelico Hall was packed recently for the jazz great, Tex Beneke and his orchestra paying tribute to the late Glenn Miller, World War II fatality. Beneke, who had been Miller's protege on the tenor sax, later became a successful band leader, but did not forget the Miller sound. The old favorites included: "Moonlight Serenade," "Chattanooga ChooChoo," "String of Pearls," "Kalamazoo" and "Miller's In the Mood."

Field Birthday

Family and old friends gathered at the home of Gertrude Ord Pollock, San Anselmo matron, to honor Jack Field, Ross pioneer, a resident of Rossmoor in Walnut Creek. His age? His old Ross school pal said they had named a freeway for him—I-80.

Jack's roots ran deep in the Sonoma-Marin area. His great-grandfather, Charles E. Field arrived in 1890 at Stewart's Point 15 miles north of Jenner, to be the first station agent and telegrapher for the newly founded Northern Pacific Railroad. He was also at Duncan Mills where his son Harry commuted by stage to Petaluma High School. Harry, his wife Helen Phair Field of Ireland, and his parents moved into Ross at the turn of the century where they resided with their children, Hazel and Jack in the two Victorian homes, side by side on Poplar Avenue. Hazel, who was married to Al Pauline, conducted the Ross Realty in the old Field home. After their demise, Jack sold to Skip Somers, a developer who turned the homes into an attractive series of shops with the name "Ross Common", which downtown Ross is now called.

Jack has two sons, Jack, Jr., member of the Corte Madera Fire Department and Michael of Petaluma. Harry Field was the first station agent at Ross for the NWP. Jack Sr. has since succumbed.

ooooo

Luck o' the Irish

Many a drama is played out in a secondhand book store. It's a great wealth of information for writers and historians and the general public who are instinctively going back to find some interesting nugget.

After dinner at Spanky's in Fairfax one evening, we sauntered down the block to see if that old store was still there. Sure enough, there stood the New Albion, with its green trim. William Bertram kindly waited on us, explaining and displaying his books, and I found myself at eye level with some books on the sea. Trying not to be rude, my eye quickly scanned them ... when what to my wondering eyes should appear ... my own grandfather's biography in its original green cover, titled *Dynamite Johnny O'Brien*, published in 1931. I had just mentioned the captain, known as "Nestor of the North", in my family story published in last week's *Junction*.

Awestruck though I was over my find, Bill Bertram had the situation well in hand. "Very often," he said, "we have this happen. Why, just last week Regan O'Brien, who is employed at 192 Broadway, sauntered in, only to discover two books written by his father, the newsman, Robert O'Brien, author for many years of the column 'Rip Tides' in the *S.F. Chronicle*."

My grandfather had been the subject of one of his stories. In another connection, Regan O'Brien was in the class of my son, Dave, at Wade Thomas School, way back in the '50's. Regan met with a fatal auto accident in 1991.

Then when I mentioned my late husband had been the building inspector in Fairfax, we were off again. "Oh, you mean Charlie Brown?!" With my affirmative answer, he proceeded to tell me the favors done for him by Charlie, who took an interest in a situation that was creating trouble for their business.

Bill's father, Harold Bertram, also owns the Mandrake Bookshop on Lincoln Avenue in San Rafael and has been in the business since 1969.

Church Series

In our series on the history of church in San Anselmo comes a letter from Mrs. Bill Ireland, who tells about the beginnings of the Marin Church of the Nazarene here.

She states, "In the early 40's, a young serviceman from Hamilton Field inserted an ad in a San Rafael paper, asking for Nazarenes in the area to form a mission.

"A San Anselman, Mrs. Rector answered the ad and together they started 'cottage church' meetings in people's homes. Herbert Coale, a charter member, brought his daughter (Verne Ireland) and his grandson (Herb Ireland) along regardless of the gas rationing during the war. Soon after they rented a storefront building on 4th Street in San Rafael, where attendance grew.

"In time, the San Anselmo Women's Club building on Tunstead Avenue became the meeting place and Reverend Chet Tolsen became the pastor. As the congregation and interest grew a lot was purchased on Sir Francis Drake Boulevard, where a small structure with living quarters for the pastor Reverend Frank Watkins was built. Many helpful hands erected a beautiful church. To increase space for its rapid growth it was enlarged under the pastorate of Reverend Hal Bonner.

"Pastors after Reverend Watkins were Thomas Betzer, Virgil Hutchinson, William Wise, Lemoine Wolf, Hal Bonner, Guy Hall, LaRolfe McCoin, Wilson Berber, Jerry Beatherage, Seldon McNutt, Dan Hopkins, Doris McDowell, Larry Smith and the Reverend James Southard.

"The Church was located for six years at the old Lansdale School, then it was moved on up to Nave Boulevard near the entrance to Hamilton Field at Novato three years ago. Since then its membership has increased four-fold, with many of the young families of servicemen at Hamilton Field in attendance. The building is once more being enhanced with added construction by the members."

C. Barron Haney, who served in the local San Anselmo post office as a delivery man and as a clerk for 30 years, and who is an elder at the church, was just honored on his 80th birthday this week with testimonials from his co-workers. His tireless efforts in anything he undertakes and his consistent kindness to the children and babies of the denomination and everywhere are his leading characteristics. Although he and wife Ruth are not grandparents, they are often taking the young parents and their offspring under their wing.

ooooo

Early Settlers camped in San Anselmo at century's turn before houses were built. Alan Moder Collection.

Camp Take It Easy

My vacation was spent at home being a good Marin citizen and re-organizing a water starved yard. The lawn was removed and drought-style plants were put in ... now watch for a downpour. Son Harry, who was just appointed executive director of the California Rural Water Association, can say a word or two about that, but being tactful, doesn't.

Camping in San Anselmo

Did you know San Anselmo was a campsite? Many early residents coming over from San Francisco would pitch tents at any available spot for the week-end or even the summer. San Anselmo Creek made a wonderful swiming hole and the hills were for hiking.

YLI History

Loretta O'Rourke, one of our ultimate pioneers, hails back to when her grandparents moved to San Anselmo after the 1906 quake. They were the Joseph Flyns that came across the bay from San Francisco with their six children, including Margaret, Loretta's mother. They bought lots on Bolinas Avenue, and camped and settled on a lot in Lincoln Park, where they did build. On the nearby property where Sunnyside Nursery is now, there was a place to swim and dance, and the residents (or campers) called it "Camp Take It Easy." The boys climbed the hills, and everyone just had a ball.

Margaret O'Rourke was later widowed and found work at Albert's Department Store. Her children, Loretta, Kay and Jo were entered into the Main School early by Miss Valerie Ansel, due to their mother's employment.

The family has long been identified with St. Anselm's Church, and Loretta, a leader in the women's group, called the YLI. That organization is to celebrate its 70th anniversary on October 26 with mass at the church, a catered brunch at the hall and a meeting later.

Loretta, a 50-year member of YLI, is chairperson of the day, and Helen Benz is in the role of chairperson. Miss Maryanna Bettencourt will preside over the meeting, and a history and review of the group will be delivered by Mrs. Alfred Lorenti. The YLI contributes to the Marin Food Bank, sells cakes at St. Anselm's festival and sells roses for Birthright, guaranteeing them $300, in addition to hundreds of philanthropies through the years.

Loretta's sister, Mrs. Bill (Katherine) Doyle lives nearby with her daughter, Kathleen, so that sisters are still close.

World Wide

Lucille Fessenden Dandelet, San Anselman, international photographer and activist and a recent winner in a national photo contest, has her work exhibited at our local Edward S. Curtis Gallery (located in the old Kaufman store).

The artist, graduate of Wellesley, and resident here since 1957, has a passion for social justice. She has been all over the globe participating in various demonstrations, such as during the 60's and 70's, she walked miles with Dr. Martin Luther King and Cesar Chavez, visited USSR in 1983 to join the first bilateral nuclear freeze demonstration in Gorky Park, and was instrumental in having San Anselmo designated as a world city, flying the UN flag for the past 20 years.

Noted Ancestors

The list reads like a *Who's Who* in boxing, the circus and even a teacher in anatomy. Mrs. John (Bobbie) Acres, who used to wave to the trainmen as a child in Lansdale, whips out names from her family that are famous and illustrious men. Her dad, Dr. Arthur B. Nelson, a ship's surgeon and anatomy instructor at College of Physicians and Surgeons in S.F., recalled having Dr. Rafael Dufficy, one of Marin's leading pioneer physicians, in his classes. It was a prestigious institution even to graduate from, let alone teach there. Bobbie's uncle George Meller was one of the greatest rough riders in the world in his teens. William Cody or "Buffalo Bill" employed him in his Wild West show along with the famous girl sharpshooter, Annie Oakley. George was known as the Arkansas Kid or Bronco George. Also her mother was married first to Tom Corbett, brother of former world heavyweight boxing champion Jim Corbett. George, the bronco buster, saw the destruction of San Francisco in the 1906 earthquake. His home, however, was in Australia.

Big Bands

Live on stage, Great Performances presented another talented duo of singers, Kay Starr and Ed Ames, to several packed audiences in two shows at Dominican's Angelico Hall recently. Miss Starr's pianist Frank Ortega rendered some of the finest jazz piano we've heard and he is also a composer of the famous "Sunset Strip" accompaniment. Rush Robinson played for Ed Ames.

Both stars presented rounded-out programs including popular as well as concert style. Marin's geriatric set, who grew up on the big band sound, were once more entertained by their kind of music.

Young and Old

How are my old and young cat assimilating to an existence together? Mai Tai, 17, who has been barely tolerating Missy, who will be a year on April 14, is now mellowing toward the younger cat and including her in a domain of protection. They are my watch cats, sailing to the window to any noise (another animal) with that usual sensitivity of cats.

ooooo

Kathrine McGovern Brown

Harry Brown

Just Among Ourselves

I've no sooner gotten my yard fixed up but will be heading off to Atlanta to see my daughter and family ... and of course the dogwood is in bloom. Need I say more? The mere mention of the South at this time of year brings to those who've been there the nostalgic sights and aromas of one of the most beautiful of growing things. However, the South is going through some of the same weather changes as Marin. For years now they have had severe droughts that are affecting trees. But the trees have another enemy ... man. They are being cut down fast enough for condos, homes, etc.

The Browns

Mr. and Mrs Harry Brown were among the first to come to San Anselmo after the San Francisco fire and earthquake. He was a native of Sheffield, England and had come in from Canada as a carpenter and builder. Among the many structures he built was St. Anselm's Catholic Church here.

Kathrine left her native Ireland when she was sixteen years old and loved to tell the story of the overland route. Especially through what is the Donner Pass when the train was held up in winter. Her Irish relatives in New York had provided her with enough food to help feed a trainload of people.

Arriving here in 1906 the couple camped on Magnolia Avenue before erecting a house on Elm Avenue which still stands. They raised two sons, Charles and Edwin (now deceased) and a daughter Alice Brown Monte, who now resides in Petaluma.

Notables Here

In our midst here is a great restaurant attraction for many notables.

It's small, has wine bottles hanging from the ceiling but the food and camaraderie of the owner, Richie, seems to give the atmosphere they are looking for. Drop-ins often are Huey Lewis, singer, Joel Bartlett and Pete Giddings, weathermen (now call naturalists) of TV station Channel 7 news, Richard Edlund, director of special effects for *Stars Wars* (winner of five Academy Awards), and his boss, George Lucas, of Lucasfilms, and Linda Ronstadt.

Richard Crispi, the owner, has been here 14 years and learned the business from his father at O Solo Mio on Chestnut Street in San Francisco. Miraculously the wine bottles did not fall in the '89 earthquake but instead would sway in one direction and then go back again. Wine bottles don't break easily. One fell from a top shelf in the cellar and bounced. His wife, Lia, formerly worked with him but his aides are now Helen Billings, Mike Hamilton, Kelly Falkin and Piage, who lives in Fairfax.

She Loves Dogs

Ann Cotta of San Anselmo not only loves animals but makes a living grooming them, mainly dogs. She turned her San Anselmo basement over to the business some years ago and does very well, dishing out love in the cleaning and drying process. It's not uncommon to see the long hair flying up under a hair dryer, or some noisy poodle being hushed with comforting sounds. She frequently has some aging animal standing by her knowing of her protection. Not a fear in the house. My two squeaky Shitsus adore her and they've been known as gate-snappers. Her mother, Mrs. Jo Cotta, is a pioneer in San Anselmo. She is a cousin of Police Chief Bernie del Santo.

Haberdasher

Orrick (Mac) McDearman was one of San Anselmo's first haberdashers. He opened his own store here after being with Wilson Brothers, a big wholesale clothing manufacturer. But his dreams were dashed with the Depression and after several more attempts he joined the staff of Albert's, Inc. His son, James, writes in his journals to us that it was then that the character of Jacob Albert was displayed. He proved to be decent and good-hearted to his merchandiser whose enthusiasm was not quenched in spite of the unfortunate economics of the day. Kaufman was the inheritor of Albert's, as Mozart Kaufman had married Albert's daughter. The firm gained a wonderful salesman in Mac who went out of his way to please a customer, even to opening up the store.

He had been named for a popular poet of the day, Orrick Johnson.

Patrick's Art

John Patrick, local artist and art supply store owner, has a photographic mind. He views a scene, goes home and makes a perfect copy of it on canvas. So he has with the Pt. Reyes seascape called *No Beginning and No End*.

Painting under the name of Jason, he has performed another lovely work, a seascape of Monterey called *Energy*, which is a close-up of waves dashing against the shore.

The Patrick Brothers, John and Paul, have conducted their successful art supply business for 31 years. They reside in Fairfax.

ooooo

Early picture of St. Anselms Church. Alan Moder Collection.

Here I Come

That Boeing 747 made a beautiful landing guided by its pilot Captain Tucker Jones over at San Francisco Airport. On a spring day when you could see forever, we skimmed over Bay waters, touching the wheels like feathers onto the ground. My window seat had allowed me to witness the sky clouds in various effects, cotton balls floating, white whipped potatoes, long layers of embossed sculpture of cloud formation casting their earthly shadows. Captain Jones gave us a tour director's guide as to what we were looking at. Poor dried out Mono Lake, center of so much controversy, but long stretches of snow covered mountains. Yosemite Park was also viewed in all its beauty.

Atlanta is being inundated with Russians (Soviet Georgians) of a friendly nature. There is a swap visit of friendship going on with Americans from the state of Georgia and those in Russia's Georgia. Both are learning about the others' country firsthand with lifelong relationships being established.

There's no place like home and with Marin in full dress of spring it is easy to see why our property has gone up and 101 is overloaded with traffic.

St. Anselm's Church

One of our best looking church edifices is the historic Victorian St. Anselm's which is located on Ross Avenue. The church and its school, a grammar school, and at one time a high school, have served the Catholics in the community well. Although keeping their religious distinctions, there has been a happy harmony in working together in most town value activities with other denominations. The nearness of locations (a block away the Presbyterian seminary) has not lessened the uniqueness of each theology of Christianity.

The building was completed in November of 1908 and was dedicated by Archbishop Riordan to Saint Anselm. The parishioners and indeed, the entire community, cooperated with fund-raising events or contributions of time and materials. As it was a branch of St. Raphael's, Reverend Riley of the parish celebrated the solemn high mass for the occasion. The first baby baptized in the new church was to later become the Bishop of Monterey, Bishop Harry Anselm Clinch.

Serving as priests through the years were the Reverends John Egan, William Cantwell, Francis Long, Patrick O'Neill, John Hayes and John Diez, Msr. John McGarr and Bishop William McDonald.

I was one of those little girls dressed in white walking down the aisle to receive first holy communion and later confirmation.

Patti M. Productions

Over three years ago a young attractive wife and mother Patti Marsh, sat in her San Anselmo kitchen drawing clever pictures on cards. Not in her wildest dreams did she imagine it would be the beginning of an international T-shirt business, nationwide and now extending into Japan.

Patti M. Productions located here in downtown San Anselmo Avenue where the old post office was. There is at work an enterprising little family group with Patti, the artist—her mother, Doris Creighton, the bookkeeper; her brother, Richard Creighton, who designed their own computer programming and printed the T-shirts; as well as Khris Waters, a family member and several others hard at it for a busy season. Patti herself does sales and marketing. She is very proud to be licensed for Earth Day Foundation and participated Sunday at Dominican. In June they will take part in the Fort Mason Earth Day exhibition.

Recently Patti drew a design of a bear and the earth for the Brookside School, which she will supply for their money-making cause. Her two little daughters attend the school. Richard Marsh, her husband of 20 years, is chief engineer of the Bank of America World. Patti's mother, Doris and father, Jack Creighton, are old Tamalpais High grads, hailing from Mill Valley originally.

I went home with some white Earth Day T-shirts and some

coloring cards and crayons to share with grandchildren. That's alright!

They have licensing agreements with Lucasfilm Ltd. for the characters in the *Star Wars* series (at Disney parks), *Willow* and the *Ewok* TV series; with Ted Turner Entertainment for *Gone with the Wind*, *King Kong*, *The Wizard of Oz*, "Tom and Jerry + Kids," "Bozo the Clown" and Save the Earth Foundation, in addition to working with major retailers, major theme parks, Disneyworld, Marine World and Yosemite Park and with major catalog houses.

ooooo

Out for a buggy ride. Two ladies of early 1900's travel down a Ross Valley road.
May-Murdock Publications.

A Treasure of Memories

Harkening back to the old horse and buggy days, Doris Schmiedell, 92-year-old resident of the Tamalpais in Greenbrae, has a treasure of memories.

Her parents, the late Edward Schmiedells, moved into Ross from San Francisco after the 1906 quake. They stayed at the Hotel Rafael while their home was being built. Her father became one of the first organizers of the Ross board of trustees in 1908 and supervised the building of the Ross roads that had to be sprinkled daily during the summer. He was founder of the Meadow Club (Fairfax) and head of the building committee.

Alice McCutcheon Schmiedell was her mother and her grandfather, Edward McCutcheon, who summered in Marin, was the only child of the Donner Party McCutcheons. He was born a year after their arrival in San Jose, escaping the rigors (and probably death) of that ordeal. He later became a prominent San Francisco lawyer. A co-founder of the Lagunitas Country Club, Alice Schmiedell disliked the Pink Saloon existing on the grounds and after its removal her husband hired architects and supervised the clubhouse building. The original tennis courts were made of Indian shells taken from nearby Indian mounds.

Painted Out Signs

Along with her friends, the Misses Sara and Natalie Coffin, Alice used to hitch up their horse and buggy and drive through Ross and San Anselmo painting out advertising signs on the fences. The family believes this was the beginning of anti-sign ordinances in the town. The Schmiedells were heavily into animals, for their children, Edward, Doris and Elizabeth owned innumerable dogs, horses, rabbits, guinea pigs and goats. They spent their childhood on horseback, on the tennis courts or driving in the spring wagon to Bolinas, stopping for lunch at Liberty's, now at the bottom of Alpine Lake.

Elizabeth's daughter, Alice Moffitt Gatterdam, raises Black Angus cattle on her Marin ranch. Doris became a working lady (for seven years at Yosemite) and enjoyed various jobs at Carmel for four years. She, along with another Rossite, Harry J. Moore, founded the Tamalpais Trail Riders to protect rights of horsemen on the Water District Trails in 1939. She was also an early director of the Babcock Foundation and Guide Dogs for the Blind. Doris claims to love Marin better the "old" way and quotes Mrs. Robert Menzies of San Rafael who said, "The rape of Marin goes on."

Bronze Sculpture

An unusual display of several Egyptian solid bronze busts by Nino Faria, San Rafael artist, can be seen at the Gold Dreams, a jewelry store in the Redhill Shopping Center here.

Mainly a surveyor in Novato, Mr. Faria is a hobbyist in sculpture and while at College of Marin where he does casting, he met Jean Jung of Fairfax, who is a jewelry designer and goldsmith. With her husband, Terry Maisel, Jung moved to San Anselmo a year ago with her business, Gold Dreams from the Cannery in San Francisco.

Mr. Faria has made a study in hieroglyphics and often makes a political statement in his work. Of mixed ethnic background, he is well-versed in other languages as well. Outstanding is his 17-inch solid bronze bust of "California Nefertitti," an Egyptian queen. On the head piece is written "Behold it was she the royal woman pretty who was Nefertitti living Goddess of the land — beautiful lady— mistress of the royal house who maketh to live in the likeness of beauty here until eternity." A smaller piece of an Egyptian pharoah, Akhnarrian, is also on display.

Other artists represented in their displays of bronze sculpture are Diane Weeks and Jean Jung of Fairfax, Blaine Black and Bill Hunt of Monterey and Scott Welles of San Francisco.

Movie in Town

Camera crews will be setting up to shoot a movie here in Creek Park on Wednesday, June 13. Also a few stores on the Miracle Mile are to be involved in it. Gloria Del Santo is closing up her Hair Express and Lisa Watroba, owner and manager of the Gold Nugget restaurant with brother, Greg Watroba, are preparing for a full day of movie activity inside their restaurant, which will be the major setting for four minutes of the film, *Sibling Rivalry* starring Kirstie Alley. The regular waitresses, Shirley, Lou, Nellie, Irene, Scottie and Pam will be serving customers while the cameras roll.

The film is being made by Castlerock Co., produced by Carl Reiner, directed by David Lester and is a comedy with star Kirstie Alley of the TV series "Cheers." There will also be scenes shot at Tamalpais Cemetery at the end of 5th Street in San Rafael.

ooooo

Horse and buggy in early 1900's on Shady Lane in Ross. Alan Moder Collection.

Breaking the Sound Barrier

We had a morning here last Monday that split the sound barrier. In other words the druggies nearby were in a loud fracas, the din created a semi-hysteria in my caged shitzus. Jackie, the vocal one, was really reacting and Toby was going on loudly.

Another neighbor heard and came running over. She called the cops. Meanwhile my piano tuner arrived and then a carpenter to alter my rooms. He announced to me that there were three squad cars in front of the druggies' home.

The carpenter started tearing apart the room. Mai Tai, the 17-year-old Siamese, had been living peacefully since the little grandchildren had been here. They are big now. But the yelling, barking and hammering were all she could bear. She ran off to see her "other mother," Clare, who lives two doors away. I got a phone call from Clare, "Guess who's here, Larine." I said, "No, not again!" But we both knew that Mai Tai needs peace and quiet!

Missy, the year-old cat is a little slap-happy and found the carpenter totally fascinating. Curiosity always overcomes her fears.

Rosie's Posies

Some homes seem to retain the personalities of their longtime occupants. So it was with the old Shearer home on Roble Court. Clara Shearer's home was her castle for 51 years until her health forced her to a nursing home at age 95. The new renter was Rosie Echelmeir of the local Marin County Flower Market, known as Rosie's Posies, on Tunstead Avenue. Clara had been an artist and her rendition of Mt. Tamalpais was of great delight to her friends. Rosie is an artist, also doing portraits in oil and water colors and conducting a business of dried and fresh flowers and instructing in floral decor with many classes.

Rosie's curiosity about Clara brought her to visiting in a local convalescent home where Clara seemed relaxed at the thought her home was taken over by an artist.

Loves San Anselmo

Rosie occupied the former Shearer home for several years and then moved back to Lagunitas where she and her son, Elias, 17, a student at Drake High, occupy a redwood home on a hillside. However, her heart remains in San Anselmo where she has attained much success in flowers and decor. A textile artist in New York for four years, she came to San Francisco and was employed by Gumps for another three years. Following her attendance at S.F. State College where she obtained her teaching degree, she taught for three years, then came to Marin 18 years ago. She has much praise for San Anselmo where she finds character and a particular tolerance that small towns show without the ethnic overload but a pleasant happy mixture. Her success with flowers is indicated by her well-attended classes of which she has conducted 40 since last October. Her students love to make garlands of dried flowers for their homes. Rosie loves her community and contributes to the decor in churches and will be decorating for the Katherine Branson graduation dinner. She annually takes part in the Renaissance Faire and is involved with the Los Angeles Fair by that name. She contributes to the Montessori School with a class of floral designing. Since moving here, the artist has integrated well into the community and her classes have become well-known.

Dallara Death

Family and friends of Louise Dallara Radieve filled St. Anselm's Church last week to pay best respects at the mass and last rites for the pioneer woman.

She was the daughter of the late San Rafael pioneers, Anthony and Mary Dallara, and had lived here at The Alameda with her husband Edward, now deceased, and son Peter for the past 40 years.

Her brother, Louis Dallara, who passed away several years ago, was a postal employee and fire department employee for Fairfax. Her son, Peter, is also in the fire department family, his wife being the daughter of San Anselmo's former fire chief Richard McLaren and Mrs. McLaren. The young folks have two young children; Gina, age 8, and Christopher, 6. They both took part in the mass for their grandmother.

Long a telephone operator and a supervisor with Pacific Telephone and Telegraph, she was a member of the company's Pioneer Club. Louise and her sisters, Enes Mager of Petaluma, Florence Curry of Carmichael, and Mary Brown of Citrus Heights, were vocal entertainers during their San Rafael High days .

Eddie Dallara of Sonoma is the deceased's brother.

Stars Entertain

Stars of the stage and screen and recording artists of fame in the persons of Connie Stevens and Glen Yarborough drew a packed audience at Angelico Hall.

Connie was born Concetta Ingolia, of Italian, Irish and American Indian descent. She came to Los Angeles as a teenager with her own group The Three Debs and was soon performing in *Finian's Rainbow*, *Rock-a-Bye-Baby* and others and played Marilyn Monroe's life for TV in "The Sex Symbol." She then toured the entire world with the show and founded a scholarship for Indian students.

Glen Yarborough's crystalline tenor voice and timeless songs held the audience spellbound. The Limelighters was his first singing group and he went from there to record 54 albums and many hit singles including "I'm a Lucky Man." He built a school for underprivileged children called SCHOLE (school for children of happiness, opportunity, love and education.)

A non-profit organization, great performances, for public benefit, presents five performances a year at Angelica Hall and Marin Center.

ooooo

A Sunday stroll in Bush Tract (now Yolanda near Center Market). Period costumes about 1900. Alan Moder Collection.

Early Founders

Let's jump on the time machine and travel back to the turn of the century. The name Lavaroni was prominent even then in the Yolanda Lansdale area of San Anselmo. John and Mary Lavaroni had come in from Boston and became large landholders at Scenic, Elm and San Anselmo Avenues. Here on this undeveloped land they had their cows, vegetable garden and large white rambling house. It was accessible to both streets and had the usual porches surrounding it. It was known as the "ranch." They became the parents of 13 children, only one of whom survives today. She is Maude Franke, 87, who resides at the Tamalpais in Greenbrae.

Back in 1906 the three youngest of the offspring, Charlie, James and Catherine "Tuddie," began the Yolanda Quality Market (where Center Market is now), along with her husband William Struckman. They were the Lavaroni Brothers and Struckman and the neighborhood grocery in those days could make or break families according to the compassion shown in tough times when money was scarce. For these good qualities, the family was known. There was also a branch of the San Anselmo Post Office located in the store with Charles serving as postmaster for five years. The store was sold in about 1953 closing another era. Charles' wife Anna was a music teacher active in the local association of music teachers. Being an ardent Catholic, at the end of her life, she joined the Third Order of Carmelite Nuns (prayer and meditation) and although living at home, upon her demise, she was laid away in a nun's habit.

Versatile Grandson

Their only son, Charles (Chuck) Lavaroni long a resident here, is now a grandfather himself. He's had a very distinguished career in the education field. A graduate of the local schools and San Francisco

State, he returned here to become principal of Isabel Cook School, thence to Novato schools and was in charge of teacher education at Dominican College.

In 1980, with two other local men, Jeff Thorner and Don Leisey, Chuck purchased a number of private schools in the Sacramento valley, Roseville, Modesto and Santa Rosa, naming them the Merryhill Schools (pre-school through elementary). These schools were recently sold by the trio. Thorner was formerly vice principal of San Rafael High School and Laisey was superintendent of San Rafael Schools.

The versatile Chuck in retirement was joined with nine other teachers in an innovative school assessment of curricula programs for the county's schools. His hobby is playing the saxophone and directing his eight-piece orchestra named Swing Society. He and wife Barbara are the parents of John, of San Francisco and Peter Lavaroni of San Anselmo and Catherine Sylvestri of Petaluma, whose husband Frank runs the Marin Products Frozen Foods in Novato. There are two grandchildren, Cara and Guilana Sylvestri. Peter and John carry on the musical tradition with their rock 'n roll band that is ten years old.

ooooo

Exciting Times

Noel Coward, the famous playwright, said in one of his poems that "mad dogs and Englishmen go out in the mid-day sun," but he didn't say anything about grandmothers with visiting offspring. Like the proverbial river, they just keep rolling along.

We had five graduation invitations and wish we could have made them all. It's an exciting time for graduates and parents who feel a sense of fulfillment as they see their youngsters walk across the stage to accept that diploma.

Emily Jean Brown, our 14-year-old, graduated from a Willits grammar school that handed out diplomas to 160. The valedictorian, Meadow Holmes, sounded like a college grad, she was that good in her public speaking. Then the next day I found myself with son Harry tooling over to Sacramento so he could conduct a seminar on the state's water (re. carcinogens) and the safety of drinking and using.

We were parked near the Department of Mental Health building, named for Gregory Bateson, the famous botanist, on Ninth Street. Inside I found a newsstand run by Richard Bromley and Dawn Hagins, both legally blind people who had the happiest camaraderie around them of understanding. Called Richard's Place the little stand sold magazines, videos and cold drinks and foods and had lots of friendliness. Richard himself claims to have been in the Department of Vocational Rehabilitation program for 17 years, having been a supervisor for two cafeterias.

And, of course, the visiting Shana Larine, 13, moved up from 8th to the 9th grade in her Marist school in Atlanta, Georgia, and is here comparing notes with her cousins. Mom Pat is along too and there is a trip to the Orient in the near offing for them. So that means ... summer sales and the "shop 'til you drop" kind of thing.

Sibling Rivalry

In the aftermath of the movie that was shot in San Anselmo, a whole role of my prints taken around the scene at the time near the Gold Nugget did not develop, sending me into a dejection. Oh well, there were three from the other that are acceptable even for pinning up on cork boards. After scooping the daily with the story and all the hullabaloo about the mega-bucks, etc. It was a great day, though, for the hard working waitresses, Nellie Williams, Lue Tabaracchi, Pam La Bounty, Irene Comer, Betty Brown, and Shirley Cole, all of whom will show in the movie *Sibling Rivalry*.

◙◙

From the porch of the 100-year-old Brown Manse here on Elm we can look back to our grandparents' days and watch the world go by as new ones constantly enter the scene. Backyard friendships kept people together and now it's come to videos for those who dislike heavy traffic ... and that other kind of traffic, the dreaded one ... drugs. Let's clean it up for the kids of the future. Remember John Kennedy's words, "Ask not what your country can do for you, but what you can do for your country." And another emphatic quote, "Say no to drugs." Wise words to heed.

◙◙

Great performances ended their series last week out at Angelica Hall with scenes and music of the '40's as they were delivered over radio stations, with antics and humor that accompanied them. Two shows were packed with grey haired seniors enjoying the oldies in the song world. The performers came down the aisles, inviting the viewers to dance, and many were accepted, providing even more merriment than ever.

Humane Dedication

This week we pay tribute to an early San Anselman, E.H. Tompkins, whose concern for animal welfare helped found the Marin County Humane Society nearly 70 years ago. Some say Miss Tompkins, whose father built the first house here (in Sequoia Park) was the 20th century equivalent of St. Francis of Assisi. She was also instrumental in founding the World Federation for Protection of Animals and in 1951 was noted by the nation's 600 humane organizations to be the nation's outstanding humane worker for animals. She maintained that compassion for dumb animals is a necessary pre-requisite to concern for one's fellow man. The dedicated woman died quietly at home at the age of 93, refusing to accept world awards personally. Her grandfather was Daniel E. Tompkins of New York, who served as vice president under James Monroe, fifth president of the United States from 1817 to 1825.

ooooo

Charles and Larine Brown were married at St. Raphaels Church July 5, 1940.

In Retrospect

Scrapbooks and photo albums are great to have but comes a time when the offspring should receive the dispersements ... that is, them that's theirs and nobody else's, or whoom! We'll all go up in smoke. I have been a lifelong candid snapper so there's plenty to go around.

However, in the looking comes reminiscing, then the nostalgia and suddenly we are pouring over all the good times and noticing the absences of two of our senior family members, namely husband and dad, Charles Brown, and my sister, Patricia, and their auntie Pat Durel-Vassar. These two people were schooled in Marin, knew most of the older families and were the eldest of three in Irish and English families. The old sod prevailed as both were trained at St. Anselm's church.

Charlie the carpenter, son of Harry and Katherine Brown, Yolanda pioneers, had a varied career as a mechanic, railroad builder, Merchant Marine sailor, ending up as a senior inspector for the Division of Architecture, State of California. Retirement bored him, so he became a building inspector for Marin towns, his last being Fairfax. Always highly respected, it was sad that he became a victim of a disease like that of Lew Gehrig with no medical cure. His demise was in May of 1989.

Sister Pat grew up in Ross and San Rafael and her comely face and long red curls made her a standout. Though married twice, there were no children so she mothered ours, David, Patricia and Harry. Her husband, Peter Durel, owned the Chevron Station in Fairfax while they resided there on Woodland Avenue. They left for Las Vegas and motel operating but upon their return to Marin Peter succumbed to a sudden illness. Pat then worked as a family aide for the county welfare (now the Department of Social Services). Like

Charles, she gave of herself greatly but human bodies having time elements, hip replacement surgery was followed by two more for adhesions (the first being unsuccessful). Then one day in August of 1988 an embolism brought sudden death. Less than one year later, Charles breathed his last on May 16, 1989.

End of an Era

An era had ended. For these families all the love, long associations, people they knew were suddenly just a memory in the minds of those succeeding them. Grandma O'Brien had said "in the midst of life, we are in death" but Shakespeare had the words for it, "parting is such sweet sorrow." Their lives had spanned the last 80 years in Marin and their memories were excellent. It was left to this writer to chronicle what she could recall or discover. It's easier after a lifetime spent doing just that.

Care to Shut-ins

Gloria Del Santo and her mobile beauty parlor, Hair Express, are licensed by the state as a pilot project. The Fairfax beautician, wife and mother of two sons, realized how much it would mean to those invalids and shut-ins to have an attendant come to their homes to style their hair.

She owns her own three chair salon Hair Express located at 2208 4th Street, San Rafael (Miracle Mile) which is open five days a week. A hairdresser for 19 years, Gloria is certified by the American Cancer Society and her van bearing her insignia is fully equipped with care necessities. In their homes or hospitals her fluctuating customers are constantly receiving her special expertise.

Gloria's cheerfulness radiates to her homebound customers and, indeed, they claim she is their ray of sunshine. Her charges are totally commensurate with what she thinks is fair and she can be reached at 457-1661.

Morning at the Vets...

It being heartworm, shot and license renewal time, we took our two dogs over for a visit to their doctor. Busy, busy were the workers and vets with the fleas and other mites coming out and dog days approaching. We especially admired Basil Rathbone the eight-month old Bassett hound of Mrs. Allison, herself expectant with twin girls, and indeed the well-behaved Basil is a faithful breed for children. The reason we know this is that Albert, my daughter's Bassett, was all tolerant of her four little ones and his untimely accidental death at age 15 was a true family loss.

ooooo

In her days as cub reporter on Marin Journal Larine began her writing career at age 19.

One Year Later

One year writing these historical anecdotes and news of the area for your *Reporter* was observed by the staff when we had a luncheon at Riccardo's last week. A spirited discussion of local media's pros and cons and "brickbats and bouquets" to get the news to you. Of course, we love it. I was reminded that I started with a cast on my broken wrist, recovering from pneumonia and my husband's death. Hardly a newcomer to Marin writing, as that began in 1935 on the old weekly *Marin Journal*. Thereby hangs another tale.

Eric Shapiro of Timothy Avenue says he always reads my column and informed me that "we're having all these problems and suddenly you come in with this beautiful insight about San Anselmo. It's just a delightful piece. I feel like I'm reading a letter." Thank you, Eric. It's been one of the many bouquets to keep us encouraged. Gracias to those who've given praise.

Who among the old-timers doesn't know the Sousas? William Sousa, retired fireman of San Anselmo Avenue, and his two sisters are the last of his generation, descendants of the late Mr. and Mrs. Antonio Sousa who arrived in the town and valley about 1878 from St. George Island.

They became extensive landowners (including a cattle ranch at the base of White's Hill) and were the parents of 13 children. One son, Frank, who had been San Anselmo's fire chief, passed on a few years ago as did his wife, Mary. A daughter still resides at the family home of Frank on Tamalpais Avenue. According to Bill, she married an officer on the "Love Boat," famous for the TV series of that name.

Bill, known affectionately by friends as Billy, was left a widower some years back and raised a large family of his own. One sister, Dorothy, lives here and another out of state. He often visits at Pinecrest with Frank's son, Antone, and family.

San Anselmo used to be a junction of rails and tracks that spread out through the county and it hasn't changed greatly except for the absence of the rails. By that I'm not discussing the traffic, which is now becoming incorrigible, but the internal functioning of the city fathers, etc. Originally called the Junction, it was given that sweet saintly pastoral name of San Anselmo. It's like a quiet little Spanish town, but like all American towns, it is a mass of ethnic groups proving its patriotism. Anything goes, in the vernacular, now. A so-called church really isn't and a small group meeting in a building really is—in that sense, that is the true meaning of the word. Webster notwithstanding.

Life goes on and unless someone comes up with a better attention-getter, it will no doubt continue.

Buon Gusta

Eleanor Giannini McCardle is one of the oldest pioneers of Fairfax, in point of residence. Her father, Fiori Giannini, established the wonderful old restaurant Buon Gusta in 1918. Eleanor continued its management after his death until 1963. It was one of the best known eateries of the area and conducted with a flair.

Goodbye

To Opal Torrance, that wonderful school nurse that served the schools and community so well in her quiet, unassuming way. She had a way of making each person feel really special, an attribute not often seen today in our rush to get ahead, etc. Opal with her kindly husband, the late William Torrance, resided for many years in the Fairfax hills, until access became impossible for the elderly couple. The couple had moved to a retirement home in Santa Cruz, leaving their beloved home with sadness. Bill's art and his Torrance Gallery were managed with the same gentility.

Animal Help

San Anselmo's contribution to the Marin Humane Society is their 30-year-old Thrift Shop open five days from Monday through Friday from 10:30 to 3:30 p.m. The auxiliary's funds have been keeping the Spay and Neuter clinic prices down for the public and to encourage pet owners to have their animals altered.

Elaine Erlinger, chairman of staffing for the shop, claims to have had 49 volunteers working in the pricing and selling the store's choice articles at low prices. Mrs. Erlinger is also historian for the Humane Society's auxiliary and Lily Livingston is its president.

The local shop is the oldest in continuity of any of a similar nature here and its workers are lifelong dedicated persons.

〜

Hundreds assembled at the Chapel of the Hills here Saturday to attend the memorial for the late Edwin E. Brown, San Anselmo pioneer who succumbed to a heart ailment in Citrus Heights.

The deceased leaves his wife, Mary; a daughter, Mrs. Charles Taylor of Duncan Mills; and a son, Edwin Brown, Jr. of San Anselmo; as well as six grandchildren and three great-grandchildren He also leaves a sister, Mrs. Alice Monte of Petaluma. His late brother, Charles, preceded him in death by two years.

ooooo

San Anselmo City Hall 1938. Alan Moder Collection.

The Way It Was

Every day became a new adventure when one's imagination was stimulated with good books or simple games and activities. Television was non-existent.

In the summer it was no more teachers, no more books, no more teachers' dirty looks—but what to do for adventure?

Well, for instance, the boys of the town took over the Kentfield slough as their swimming pool, and they all went there—skinny dipping—no girls allowed. The slough was located from the area between Marin College bookstore and Marin Catholic High School, non-existent at the time.

Curiosity took over little Sis and I one day, and we began edging around there, little realizing the deep, dark secret that was involved. Big brother came out and told me to go *home!* There was a warning edge to his voice that was adamant. I obeyed reluctantly but didn't understand the full portent until later.

Old Cordone Gardens

Can you picture the truck garden run by Joseph Cordone from 1890 to 1926 on the property where Drake High stands?

The Cordones owned 1.5 miles of the land and surrounding acres. Their produce was shipped all over Marin and Sonoma with the employment of 33 workers. Joe had come from the Piedmont section of northern Genoa and his wife, Rose, came from the Italian Riviera. They later met here and were married. They were the parents of four girls and three boys, only one of whom remains, the eldest, Marius (Mack) Cordone, of San Rafael. The last surviving sister was Miss Eva Cordone, of the old family home across from Drake High on Sir Francis Drake Blvd. She succumbed last year at 91. Employed by Rosenburgs, a dried fruit firm in San Francisco for 32 years, she spent much of her time across the Bay. When she did return home on the late train and step off at Yolanda Station to walk home in the dark, it was not with the trepidation there is now.

Market Street

At one point the Cordones were ordered to put in streets of six-inch concrete and three-inch asphalt (more than is on Market Street) at a cost of $35,000. Inner roads were made of gravel from the creek, steam rolled and watered down. The property included Saunders Avenue.

Mack claims he had picked out a 2,600-acre ranch in Napa for his father to buy after his graduation from U.C. Davis. However, the concrete costs changed that plan. He became a Marin realtor instead.

The Cordone property was sold to the Tamalpais High School District in 1940. However after the large gardens were discontinued, others were kept up, one on Saunders Avenue, one at Sleepy Hollow and one near St. Vincent's School for Boys in San Rafael.

A one-acre orchard exists on the grounds of the original homestead in San Anselmo where Miss Cordone lived. She urged me to come over and borrow her high-reach tree picker when I told her how productive our 40-year-old pear tree was.

The Quinn Family

The Arthur Quinn family of Magnolia Avenue here were a close-knit and productive group. Alma and the twins, Artie and Ninny as everyone knew them, were fine athletes through their lives and spent much time coaching the youth of the community. Their true names, Arthur and Frank, were seldom used. The boys, identical twins, had excelled in baseball in school and became semi-pro ball players. But always they became involved in either coaching or refereeing for youth games. Their sister, Alma was a founder of the San Anselmo Tennis Club and was most active in teaching the children. She was married to Wesley Swadley, a successful photographer. The couple were childless but were always teaching the young.

Mr. Quinn, Sr., was a local postman as were his sons. His wife Elvira was a gourmet Italian cook and often during their lives the family returned for lunch at Mama's.

That generation of the family are all gone, the three, Alma, Artie and Ninny, having succumbed in the early '70's. However, their widows, Irene Quinn, of San Anselmo, and Rosalind Quinn of San Rafael remain, each of them having two children.

Arthur Quinn, Jr., is the author of two books, one of which, *The Broken Shore* is the history of Marin Peninsula, an intellectual treatise on the topography and culture of Marin since early days. One of his statements, no doubt biblical, struck us: "One generation passeth away and another generation cometh, but the earth abideth forever. "

ooooo

San Anselmo train depot. Alan Moder Collection.

We Rode the Rails

Did you ride the Tam High Special? The question drew my immediate response, "Did I ever!" Who could forget the station to station daily pickup of students attending Tamalpais High School from Ross Valley by the Northwestern Pacific Railroad? There were three cars carrying about 85 students each plus two regular passenger cars in a train pulling out a 8 a.m. on weekday mornings. A picturesque and memorable part of our lives. They ran from 1920 to 1940 when they ceased and students had to take buses. Just when they were badly needed and we had a boom, the trains were discontinued in 1941. Wooden cars were on the tracks from 1920 and later interspersed with steel cars in 1930 when Santa Fe Railroad was bought out. Regular passengers went on to board the SS Eureka from Sausalito to San Francisco. That mammoth ferry was built at Hunter's Point and christened the SS Ukiah and was the oldest in the world until its dry dock days where it is at the Maritime Museum.

The Discovery Shop of the American Cancer society which left Greenfield Avenue here to move up to 2nd and A Streets, San Rafael, is filled with gently used items of miscellaneous variety. According to Diane Salinger, development director of the ACS, the shop is staffed by 45 volunteers, many of whom have had cancer among their friends or families. For 12 years it was located here in San Anselmo. On Monday we dropped in to find their low cost books were half off and we purchased a lovely oil of Lake Tahoe, a real Travis, popular local artist. Volunteers there were Ellie De-Martini, Jacine Parker and Lois Rose of San Anselmo, and Pat Haskell, Margaret Farley and Dorothy Grehm of San Anselmo.

The county has three Discovery Shops, identified by the large blue awnings circling the building.

Surprise

A surprise birthday celebration was recently in honor of Mrs. Marty (Frances) Moder, San Anselmo pioneer. The local matron, mother of four grown sons and eight grandchildren underwent heart surgery twice in nine months. Her successful recovery was attributable to the many friends who prayed and her own strong faith and love of people. Her husband, Marty, a builder, succumbed four years ago and was a member of the Sons of Retirement. The family for years spent their summers camping and fishing in the northern Dunsmuir area.

The Storeroom

Susan's Storeroom at 239 San Anselmo Avenue here is in its 16th year of operation and increasingly popular.

Susan Hoy, the young manager, likes to talk about her shop's beginnings in the basement of the old Modesta Pinza home on Tunstead Avenue, which she had purchased 16 years ago. A single parent, she was also raising two little boys then. The older, Chris, has just graduated from Marin Catholic High School where he was elected most valuable ball player. He will be entering Chico State in the fall. His brother Danny is a student at Marin Catholic.

You couldn't miss the store. It has a gigantic bear seated out in front.

Deja Vu

Emily Dvorin, manager of Various and Sundries for 17 years, has taken over the left side of the ground floor in the old Home Market building. During the refurbishing of the 1,100 square feet, there was discovered marble and tile work left from the days of the old Home Market and that of Gabriel Franchini. The tile of superior quality and design was ordered from Scotland and took months to arrive, according to Bill Franchini, the owner's son. The floor has a black pattern running through, and the marble shelves were originally butchers' cutting tables. Mrs. Dvorin's fixtures are of wood, accentuating the lovely tile work.

Lillian and Harry Brown of Willits attended the wedding of David and Dana Burnett recently at the Marin Art and Garden Center. Lillian is managing editor of the *Willits News* and Harry is executive director of the California Rural Water Division.

Harry and David grew up here together, going to Wade Thomas School, Drake High School, Dave to the Dominican School of Music and Harry to Cal Poly in San Luis Obispo.

ooooo

Capt. O'Brien's early command of the Alden Bessie on the Oriental trade route. One of the early clippers, the ship was attacked by Chinese pirates as it left Hong Kong. Capt. O'Brien, Larine's grandfather, easily escaped them. This and other tales appeared in his autobiography.

A Life Well Spent

Life goes on, amidst the worst storms at sea, typhoons, iceberg warnings and catastrophes of many kinds.

By popular demand, I'll continue the story of the dynamic sea captain who was my grandfather, Captain John A. O'Brien. His biography, any news clippings and personal stories related over his captain's table may have changed the behavior of people a great deal. Rex Beach, noted author, placed him in the role of Captain Brennan in his famous novel. Jack London was totally inspired by his awesome true life experiences. *Sea Wolf* was born in concept at such a gathering.

We are constantly reading about the sea in many ways. If we can survive the dangerous waters we are lifted to a calm sea. So it was literally for Captain Johnny, who was my father's dad. He spent a lifetime proving this.

Heroism at Sea

His heroic maritime behavior included the saving of the stranded Umatilla on a sand bar with another sailor. Two days with crackers and water aboard her at Coos Bay in 1898 was sufficient to rescue the ship for its owners. Ripley had to mention it in "Believe It or Not", for the perseverance shown under grinding circumstances.

Then in 1895, Lewis and Drydens *Maritime History of the Northwest*, published in Portland about sea adventurers, told of John A. O'Brien, a well-known shipmaster of the Pacific Coast for many years, plying between Columbia Bar, Puget Sound, San Francisco and China afterward entering the steamship service in the Northwest. He knew the dangers and glories of the Inside Passage, the sheltered island-studded route from Seattle to Skagway and soundly re-buffed the crested roller prevailing out westward in the gulf of

Alaska. This country O'Brien never tired of but was always aware of hidden pinnacles of rock waiting beneath the surface to rip bottoms out of ships.

Knowledge of the Waters

His ship would crawl past the great glaciers and ice bluffs and her decks would heave when a descending berg dropped off into sea, sending circles of waves.

Ketchkin, Sitka, Petersburg, Skagway, Juneau, Carova, St. Michael and Noma. All knew O'Brien and he knew them. He knew the waters of Clarence and Prince William Sound as he knew his own cabin, the dangerous, half-hidden ice menace, which made navigation in the Bering sea notorious.

What would grandfather say if he were alive today about the Valdez oil spill in the beautiful Prince William Sound and the revolting consequences?

"No man worth his salt leaves his bridge for any reason whatsoever"?

Apologies

Dave and Teresa Stoner of Fairfax, please forgive us for the gremlins getting into the story about daughter, Elizabeth last week. Already a cover girl having had her photo on a magazine cover, her parents are two clever people in horticulture and floral design.

Also Mrs. E.A. Burnett's name was omitted from the story of her son's wedding very inadvertently. A most kindly person and modest, but it really was sent in.

ooooo

Legacies

"Over there ... over there. Say a prayer for the boys over there ... " is the nostalgic tune that returns to many as it seems that 1940 and/or 1955, the wartime years, are back all over again. The boys handsome in their uniforms are saying goodbye to their loved ones as they embark for the Persian Gulf. There, according to news, the new generation is to take on the Mid-Eastern world for America. Our opposition to Saddam Hussein's capture of all the oil fields for Iraq is leaving us precariously on the edge of war.

About 20 of our close draft-eligible youth may be called.

Antiques

The Legacy Antiques (formerly Hunter's Depot) at 204 Sir Francis Drake Boulevard here is a cool place to browse on a warm afternoon. We were looking for small end tables and found one to our liking. All kinds of old pictures, prints and postcards, 1940 radios, tables, chairs, chests, china closets are there for the asking. We came across an old copy of the weekly *Marin Journal* of April, 1900, and it brought back memories. My late mother, Agnes O'Brien, had been the editor before her demise. I was given the old *Journal* literally to teethe on (that's where I did my first newswriting at age 19). The paper was the oldest in California with prestige until it was bought out by the *San Rafael Daily Independent*. The old *Journal* was established in 1861, Jerome Barney was editor, and it was owned by the Olmsted Brothers. Besides the Boer war and other national issues, much feature space was given to the cure of children's diseases, such as croup, whooping cough and measles.

Legacy Antiques is currently owned by Roger and Sabrina Daniels of San Anselmo.

More Old Things

Old leather bound books, oriental rugs and antique objects de art fill the store called Showcase Antiques, located on San Anselmo Avenue where Kaufman's store formerly was.

Anthony McNaught, an English authority on such things, is the store's owner and his recent bride, Dawn Kirchner McNaught, is his co-worker. The McNaughts both have an excellent background in such dealings. Anthony received his early training at Christie's House, an auction place in London where he took classes in fine arts and worked in auctions. His bride was an antique dealer in Los Angeles and Hollywood.

An entire workshop for the restoration of old items, books, leather, etc. is located in the rear of the store. McNaught has great expertise in leather restoration. He studied the decay of leather and how it can be arrested. He claims this is an area of increasing interest. The lovely art works are European and American.

The couple was married at St. Vincent's Church in Marinwood at a formal wedding on June 25, 1990.

Mrs. Gassner

Mrs. Jo (Lillian) Gassner, longtime resident of Sir Francis Drake Boulevard here, is an extremely active person with many friends and hobbies. This has recently been curtailed, however, by a fractured ankle, incurred while walking down a San Francisco street. She fell when her heels went out from under her and she clung to a light pole, saving further injury.

The popular localite, when not going to the horse races or swimming at S.F. Marine Memorial Club, is frequently writing cards to friends, many times the ill or the shut-ins.

McCarthys

Nick and Dan McCarthy left here 26 years ago to purchase a ranch at Granada (near Eureka). The couple joined their daughter, Patty and husband, who later moved on to Grant's Pass where he became an accountant. The couple have enjoyed the outdoor farming life, riding horses, etc., and are now living in Redding. They ran Mack's Photo for 30 years, which is a block up from the current post office.

They had first lived at the senior McCarthy's home on Belle Avenue before purchasing the building where the photo company now stands. Dan had been a guard at San Quentin Prison before joining his wife in the business.

They were bought out by Tom Rygh, who owns the North Bay Photo and publishes a series of real estate publications. Ruth Williamsen of Fairfax formerly managed Mack's, where she had been an employee of the McCarthys.

Hazardous Crossing

An ambulance followed a fire engine by the Bank of America across from the Wells Fargo Bank at that busy intersection one day last week. Luckily it wasn't a busy traffic time and cars were diverted down Tunstead Avenue or there might have been a major congestion. The crosswalk between the two banks is often unheeded with heavy speed through that area. The villagers know one false step there could mean disaster.

ooooo

Ross Station was a busy spot in 1910 for train travelers coming and going. Harry B. Field, the trainmaster, was an early pioneer. Roy Farrington Jones Private Library.

Where the Boys Were

The Ross kids and their San Anselmo counterparts weren't so different at Halloween some 50 years ago. A few seniors like to recall their miscreant days of misbehavior on the big night. An occasion at the Ross Post Office had every federal agent investigating how the four chickens were found running around inside the day after. Or how Mr. Molenkamp's cow ended up in the Ross train depot or why the Chinese vegetable wagons were hanging up on top of the station building. Gates ended up on the tops of cars so often that owners removed them first. The one cop in each town would throw up his hands and say "Boys will be boys." In those days they didn't worry about the drugs and violence department. Everyone was known and held accountable. Newcomers were viewed with suspicion unless proven okay.

Bud Walsh's father and Clayton Stocking were the successive keepers at Phoenix Lake in Ross. Along with the Molenkamps, they loaned out horses to the admiring boys of the area and would pay them ten cents to walk them into town. My brother, Mick, cared for "Nellie," one of the mares one summer, an unforgettable time. She'd get angry and let fly, kicking the slats out of our barn. Somehow the country stayed with Mick, and he got his degree in animal husbandry at U.C. Davis, later owning a large sheep ranch in Williams. In between he had served nearly four years in the Army's Pacific theatre of war.

The Pringle family on Butterfield Road had horses and Ed Brown cared for one of these. His love for them led him to be an excellent rider and later winner in local horse shows. His own horse, "Apple" was kept in his horse barn on Salinas Avenue at which time he became an active member of the Marin Sheriff's Posse.

Swing Society

Chuck Lavaroni, a pioneer of Yolanda here, is living proof that life doesn't end with retirement. He went from one love to another as he retired as a public school educator. He went full time into his band conducting with the Swing Society that features the "Big Band" sound of yesterday. His background in education reads like a *Who's Who*. He was a public school administrator for 18 years in San Anselmo, Novato and Sausalito. Prior to retiring in 1982, he served on the Dominican College staff as director of elementary teacher education program and as Dean of Admissions and Financial Aid.

His Swing Society has become popular around this area. They will appear Saturdays, on November 3 and December 1 at the Marin Solos dance at Isabel Cook School, and on alternate Fridays at Rancho Nicasio. All are welcome to attend.

Lynn Giovanniello, the band's only female member, is a bass player. She has performed at the local college symphony and with Marin-Light Opera. Hailing from New York and Florida, she taught music many years at Reed School District in southern Marin while husband Ralph was its superintendent. They currently operate two private schools in Santa Rosa.

Another pioneer San Anselman, Bernie Lussier, is the piano and keyboard player and the music arranger. He is the organist at the First Presbyterian Church in San Anselmo. The drummer, Frank Lakeman, is a native of Canada, a resident of San Rafael for 47 years and a water district retiree.

Chuck Lavaroni's family owned much of the property on Scenic and Elm Avenues in the early years. His grandparents had a small farm and ran a local grocery store. His mother, the late Anna Lavaroni, was a leading Marin music teacher.

Theatrics in Schools

There's a bevy of children coming out of the San Anselmo-Fairfax school systems already trained in music and arts thanks to the cooperation of local parents, teachers and families, in spite of the federal funds cutback. For ten years now a cooperative miracle has been executed in the five productions a year which are so close to professional.

One of these was the four performances of the musical hit comedy, Cole Porter's *Anything Goes*, performed at the Marin Community Playhouse on Kensington Road in San Anselmo over the previous weekend. The sophisticated lyrics and music accompanied fast stepping dancing in many old classics. A packed house turned exuberant with applause at the excellence in the performances. Rightfully so as the character parts had been diligently practiced.

It was the parents' production of the Ross Valley Community for Schools, inclusive of White Hill School, Manor, Brookside, and Wade Thomas. This is all to finance the fine arts in these schools since federal funding had failed. Codirectors were Michael A. Berg and Sandi V. Weldon, assistant Kay Coleman. Music director was Kelvin McNeal and assistant Lynne Davies. Weldon was also choreographer and played the lead role of Reno Sweeney, a bar entertainer who fell in love with an English lord, Sir Evelyn Oakleigh, played by Jay Murphy.

During intermission a repast was provided for the milling crowd as they socialized with the actors and workers.

Parents and teachers keep costs down by making all costumes, scenery and providing chaperons for the parties as well as refreshments. Weldon came here about eight years ago from the east where she obtained her college masters in theater as a dance teacher and choreographer. In addition to conducting classes at College of Marin she has been an integral part of these performances, directing them as well as the individual school plays. With great vigor and interest and continual activity in the cause she has had tremendous results. The children are absorbed and cooperative and many have gone on to higher schools with theater foundation useful in their future lives.

ooooo

Downtown San Anselmo in 1935 showing the Cheda building housing the drugstore. This was formerly the Strand Theatre first Marin theatre showing films by way of an arc lamp. Roy Farrington Jones Private Library.

San Anselmo's Architectural Heritage

Good speakers, wonderful dinner in a fine setting greeted the members and guests of the San Anselmo Historical Commission here October 24.

Held at Alexander Hall on the grounds of the San Francisco Presbyterian Theological Seminary, many of the pioneers were able to go out on the deck to admire the fall colors. Then a gracious meal was presented to the locals followed by a slide show of significant San Anselmo buildings.

The presentation was made jointly by Dan Goltz, a San Anselman and architect of Creek Park, and Louis "Skip" Stewart, lecturer, photographer and past town councilman.

Buildings described for their architecture before and after were Sir Francis Drake and San Anselmo Avenue; the Hub intersection; Creekside Park before and after Larkspur barricade; Wells Fargo Bank and Cheda building in 1969; Mt. Baldy and the Seminary; Tunstead Avenue (before the Wells Fargo bank); Sir Francis Drake toward Red Hill, same view today; Orrick Travel (built in 1910) originally the First Bank of San Anselmo (done in Greek Temple style when banks were "temples" so people would feel money is safe); 10 Bank Street, built in 1912 and originally Grosjean Market (the first commercial building in San Anselmo to have a full basement); and the Farrington Jones Building, a mixture of many classic elements indicative of personal architecture with use of stained glass.

Also, the Tamalpais Community Theatre, built in 1923, shows a highly decorated baroque to Egyptian (also eclectic mission style with deco). Grammar schools held their graduation exercises here and the first movie to play was *The Hummingbird*, with Gloria Swanson. The Cheda Building was built in 1912 at a cost of $16,000 and originally was called the Strand Theatre. The Strand was the first movie theatre here and showed silent films via an arc lamp projector. The light could be seen around the town. The exterior was in rustication with painted brick, detailed shields and family emblems and heavy cornices at both ends. Also the Italian Pallazzo architecture was shown with the well-proportioned windows. Many slides were shown of the buildings, old and new.

The building presently housing the Wells Fargo Bank was originally the American Mercantile Trust and was built in 1926. The temple front with clock and baroque scrolling and garlands (railings) denotes an eclectic version of the Italian Pallazzo design, originally in stone, now in brick, and the rusticated cornices.

Home Market building, one of the first buildings in San Anselmo, had been owned by G. Franchini. A meat, produce and general market, it had literally grown with the town, and slides were shown with the old Tin Lizzies parked in front. Today it is occupied by a series of shops. The exterior facade gives a Spanish look (stucco) but with Arabesque details (balconies). Following pictures of the San Anselmo railroad and power station, or junction, a series was shown of Montgomery Chapel built in 1896 by Saunders and Wright for the San Francisco Theological Seminary. Funds are now being raised to refurbish this building. Its style, typical of the turn of the century, is of a small French Abbey church, graced with Tiffany windows. The structure served as the backdrop for a silent film version of *Faust*, with John Barrymore.

The Seminary's historic Scott Hall was built in 1892, named for the Seminary's first president, built of local stone, basalt and San Jose sandstone. Geneva Hall is of cast concrete made to simulate fine stonework. Round arches are Romanesque, painted in Gothic with a touch of the Spanish.

Other buildings shown and described were the Bauer building, the decco of the old post office, an old gas station and San Anselmo downtown in years past and present.

ooooo

Hope Springs Eternal

These are busy days and those who didn't bother to vote shouldn't complain. Voting has become a very important freedom left to us. If we do our duty, then the elected should be the right choice.

Americans are allowed their dreams and ruminating, finding comforts in simplicities. After a two weeks' depressing bout with the flu, the words came to me, "The day's at the morn ... God's in his heaven. All's right with the world." As the words penetrated my brain, I had to confide in my friend, Stella, a versatile linguist, intellectual and Christian. If she doesn't know the answer, she looks it up. Sure enough, it was something from Robert Browning called "Pippet Passes", e.g., "The year's at the spring/and day's at the morn/morning's at seven. The hillside's dew-pearled, the lark's on the wing/snail's on the thorn/God's in his heaven/all's right with the world."

In our creative moments, unobstructed by the world's furies, we are by nature a positive people ready to surge ahead in spite of defeats. How did a spring poem enter on the verge of winter? Hope springs eternal if left to our own devices. This area is a true paradise, the leaf colors are a brilliant hue, and the trees valiantly carry on in the drought. San Anselmo vistas are breathtaking. At the main intersection we see the brilliance of autumn trees in Creek Park, topped by the Seminary spires, at the foot of our Mt. Tamalpais. An unequalled sight in our midst ... no wonder new people are attracted, but we remember our ancestors who trod those roads and before that the Indians were hunting bear.

⁕

Out of a booklet called *The Quake of '89* as told by San Anselmo schoolchildren, we selected the work of Brian McGee of Ms. Andrews' third grade at Brookside School.

"On October 17, 1989, my mom and I went to San Francisco to see the third game of the World Series. It was a hot day in San Francisco. It was very crowded.

"At five o'clock the ceremonies began. As planes started to fly over us, everything started to shake. The chairs were going back and forth. People started to yell. 'Earthquake!' My mom and I got up and ran down the steps. They were cracking. We looked up and saw the sky through the cement ceiling.

"When we got to the parking lot, there was a man in a limousine watching the news. Mom asked if we could use his telephone to call home. The buses could not get out of the parking lot. We asked some people if they lived in Marin. They said they would give us a ride home. They did not have much gas so we had to stay until 12:30 a.m. and have someone follow us home. We got there at 2:30 a.m.

"The next day we read the newspaper and found out that we were in the most damaged section of Candlestick Park. We also found out that a lady sitting four seats behind us had cement fall on her head. We were so glad to be home! "

⌁

Our seniors seem to enjoy the music they grew up with and swarm into Angelico Hall in San Rafael where Great Performances brings in leading musicians. It was so last Thursday night when Pete Fountain's swinging clarinet delivered music that was the sound of Bourbon Street in New Orleans. As a nine-year-old boy with bad lungs, Peter Dewey LaFountain, Jr. hung around legendary jazz clubs, hoping to become a drummer. The family doctor advised the clarinet for his lungs and this started his meteoric rise to fame. After being with some of the best known Dixieland bands, he spent two years on the Lawrence Welk show and ended up in Carnegie Hall. He has recorded 80 albums, three of them are gold and he has made command performances before four presidents and Pope John Paul II.

Also on the program were the Limelighters, often associated with the early 60's when the trio became one of the best known folk groups in America. They skillfully blend both old and new into a unity of music, humor and a kinship with the audience.

ooooo

Thompkins estate and Victorian home originally built in 1869 and later sold to George Lucas. San Anselmo Historical Commission.

'Tis the Season for Celebration...
Begin Early at Tour de Noel

It's looking a lot like Christmas down in Ross as preparations are under way for St. John's Church annual house tour and boutique on Saturday, December 8 from 10 to 4 p.m.

Last Wednesday a gaggle of press persons was exposed to the delightful homes on this year's tour. Luncheon was served high up in the Kent Woodlands hills, where Mt. Tam seemed an arm's-length away and could be viewed from many rooms. Volunteers Mini Burton of Kentfield, Jan Grimes of San Rafael, Jan Heglund of Fairfax, Pam Schaefer and Suzanne Mellor of Kentfield tended to every detail of this delightful press preview occasion.

The press corps guests consisted of Beth Ashley, Marin *Independent Journal*; Delsa Ham, editor of *In Marin* magazine, Jorie Parr of *Marin Messenger* in Mill Valley, and yours truly, one of *Marin Scope's* feature editors as well as historian.

Our preview tour began at the former home of Dr. Allen Hinman in Ross, built in 1946. The current owner is a student of culinary arts, an interest reflected in her comfortable kitchen, which was done in oak and brick by Janean for the owner 20 years ago. Blue and white colors set a background for the traditional home while country antiques were prolific about the home. Brick terraces overlook the pool, while a tiled fireplace and half-canopy bed dominate the master bedroom. One standout was a special display of the works of Beatrix Potter dating from 1898 donated by her mother. Upstairs is a "male retreat" with books, a fireplace and many collections of antique fly rods, cars and model planes especially for the man of the house.

Ducks, rabbits, geese and lambs are a predominant theme in her daughter's bedroom. There was a large array depicted in pottery in the unique girl's peach-colored room. Her cat "Fluff-button" followed us from room to room.

Old Ross

From there we drove over to Lagunitas Road to the 1906 home built as a summer place by a San Francisco family. Here we found a most creative couple displaying their heritage pieces with modern and international travel items done up in charming ingenuity. Rare antiques and Victorian family furniture are mixed in a manner to display the original home design of the occupants.

⊱━⊰

Down the street we visited a home with an English Tudor exterior, but upon entrance the visitor finds a Southwestern Villa with salmon-colored Mexican tiled floors, antiques and contemporary art pieces and furnishings, all well integrated. The house is double its original size now and shows a truly livable combination of light walls, spaciousness and old country design. On display are a replica of the 90-foot power yacht and a 40-foot sailboat.

Mt. Tam View

A lovely conclusion was a tour of a home high up in the Kent Woodlands hills that is not to be forgotten. The master bedroom has an enclosed spa area with a roll-back roof and a large shaded deck with close-up view of Mt. Tam. The living room has a similar view with "round the Horn" antiques that were their grandparents'. Off the blue and white kitchen is a separate all-glass breakfast area in hexagonal shape. A spiral staircase is enclosed in an all-glass turret leading down to a pool and barbecue area. The intimate wine-tasting room with cork-lined walls, guest room, TV viewing room, and game room prove the home to be spectacular throughout. The view was obviously their theme, as it is awe-inspiring.

Grandma's Cupboard

The December 8th house tour will be accompanied by a boutique and Grandmother's Cupboard at the Ross Church. There will be a sale of wreaths, topiary trees, linens, porcelain dolls, hand-painted sweatshirts, ornaments, stocking stuffers and Christmas gifts. A special item will be a custom-designed Amish whole cloth quilt of antique muslin, quilted by members of St. John's to be offered in a raffle. Grandmother's Cupboard will feature traditional holiday foods, including mustards, chili sauce, relishes and breads.

Shuttle service to many beautiful Ross Valley homes on the tour and return to the church's boutique and lunch are provided by the many volunteers at the public price of $20.00. St. John's Church is located at the corner of Lagunitas Road and Shady Lane in Ross.

Proceeds benefit the church's outreach programs (Human Concerns) including Canal Ministry in San Rafael, the Ecumenical Convalescent Home Ministry, and the St. John's Emergency Fund at the Marin Department of Social Services office.

We would highly recommend this little Christmas-in-Ross event for a nominal fee (contribution to Marin's needy).

Save yourself a trip abroad and come see Ross Valley's finest at Christmas.

🙼🙽

The annual Christmas Boutique of the Catch-All Shop at 541 San Anselmo Avenue here will be held from Tuesday, November 27 at 10 am through Christmas.

The shop is sponsored by the Branson School of Ross which is a college preparatory high school with grades nine through twelve. It is an outgrowth of the "Closet" that was available to the students who needed to replace their uniforms, most often a blue gingham frock. Older students would donate their outgrown garments for the use of younger ones. This tradition evolved three years ago into the local shop which contains all sorts of items gently used by their previous owners.

🙼🙽

Gertrude Ord Pollock, our local matron with the tremendous Oak in her yard, is a plucky one. Following her second hip surgery, pneumonia and pleurisy, she is back at her wheel and her social life is an extensive one. Lots of friends and plenty of spirit.

⊫⊣

As you all probably know, San Anselmo was known as The Junction before the turn of the century, because it was a center for the railroad trains as they departed into different directions. Trains are an integral part of our history, so much that an early picture usually showed a train or station in it.

ooooo

Holiday Happenings

Nothing really quenches the excitement of Christmas time when the gift giving is paramount. Not war, or rumors of war, earthquakes, fires or dire predictions of repressions. The loss of loved ones becomes more poignant with memories, but time is a healer.

We've noticed an increased demonstration of togetherness as a people, which is the American birthright. Old friendships and relationships are being restored, reunions with relatives after many years of broken ties become apparent. When faced with possible war the human condition goes back to survival.

Party

We were treated to a wonderful Christmas luncheon last week at the home of Verne Ireland here. An old-fashioned sing of the Christmas carols around the piano over which Mrs. Ireland presided and a delightfully appointed table for the dispensation of refreshments was enjoyed by all.

This is an annual custom for the hostess whose late husband, Bill Ireland, was a leading builder in the county.

Grandma's Cupboard

We were happy to loan my late sister Pat's lovely Hutch (cupboard) to the St. John's boutique and Grandma's Cupboard event that was given in conjunction with the Tour de Noel tour of homes in Ross. Last year the event brought in $10,000 to be donated to Outreach programs in Marin County. Mimi Sutton was the able chairman over a large volunteer staff.

<hr/>

Right smack in the middle of Christmas shopping last week the gear on my new car refused to work, stranding me by the Bank Pharmacy in Fairfax. After repeated calls to my car agency, vague answers, wrong numbers, I was forced to use a pay phone, then ran out of dimes and patience. I finally rose up with my Irish and informed them a tow truck was now overdue and pronto, it appeared. So did a loaner car, which my agency is paying for due to the warranty on my new car. Shopping was held up a few days but the squeaky wheel gets the grease.

⊷⊶

He could write a book. My brother John A. O'Brien, III, of Petaluma, spent four years in the Pacific theater in 1940-44, New Guinea in particular. The enemy hid out in caves or took potshots from the trees, which meant kill or get killed. The 142nd outfit in which he was a "sarge" had many honors given at the end of the war. His good conduct medal also meant he was good at survival. The former veteran was in the sheep and rice ranching business with Clinton Jewett, his U.C. Cal Davis fraternity brother, in Williams for many years, and has many friends in Colusa County, as well as Marin where he was raised.

⊷⊶

Ken and Mary Ball just returned from Carmel with their 15-year-old cat, Samantha. They were there for eight days and found their favorite person, Kim, had married the famous photographer, Edward Weston, who is on a par with Ansel Adams, in fine photography.

History in Buildings

Members of the San Anselmo Historical Commission heard a speaker from the local seminary last week.

Patricia Bulkley, of Kentfield, a chaplain and trustee on the San Francisco Presbyterian Theological Seminary, discussed the need for restoration of the 100-year-old Montgomery Chapel.

She said there are so few buildings that size with the acoustics so perfect that in restoration it might also be used as an inter-faith chapel. An Oakland foundation, Hedco, has promised to contribute

$800,000 toward the restoration of Montgomery Hall but the remainder of the $1.6 million project must be raised.

It would be made earthquake safe and the 12 stained glass windows would be reinforced. Pictures of the beautiful windows done in 1890 Tiffany style were displayed by the speaker. An engineering committee is now examining it and three architects are to bid.

On the committee are William B. Murray, San Rafael Banker, Joanne Dunn, founder of the Marin Arts Council, and Roger Poore, former mayor of Ross.

The local commission meeting was presided over by Katharine Coddington of Ross. There was discussion of a home tour of leading San Anselmo homes to be held next year. Ms. Coddington reported that over $300 came in from sale of the schools' earthquake books, compiled by children's personal descriptions of the 1989 earthquake. Bill Franchini, treasurer, told of the group's finances and Pat Swensen stated the October dinner at the Seminary was a large success. Bill Davis announced that a contribution of old newspapers was made by William Hill.

The group meets on the 3rd Wednesday of January in the Museum beneath the public library.

No Room at The Inn

The First Baptist Church here was turned into the Bethlehem Inn for a Christmas dinner and Nativity play.

The Bethlehem Inn, performed first by the Contemporary Drama Service in Colorado, is a dinner play for Christmas with the audience as part of the cast.

During the dinner, Eli, the Innkeeper (Rev. Paul Keeler, pastor of the church) and a cast of 12 dressed in Bedouin costumes enacted the scene of No Room at the Inn and the Birth of the Christ Child. Effective as his wife, Sarah, was Earline Barron. Joseph and Mary were in the persons of the Rev. James Southard of Church of the Nazarene and his wife, Frieda Southard. Servants were Betty Jo and Randy Kinsell, Martin Robrecht, and Fay Cottingham. Shepherds were Mindy Duncan and Peter Paolina, while the children's parts were taken by Jamie and Jo Ann Southard and Matthew Kinsell.

Ellora Meyer directed the play and Beverly Keeler was chairman of the dinner volunteers. The program ended with a soprano solo by Mrs. Brett McCarty of "O Holy Night."

Christmas

Christmas entered into our hearts
His birth so amply rewarding.

His Holy Spirit broke ramparts
The highest power recording.

Revealing God's promise and love
In the birth of a tiny babe.

In Bethlehem with stars above
He brought His mercy mild,

Son, He proved of a sovereign king
Royalty ... born in a stable.

To all, His blessings to bring
How much that He is able.

Men were given a joyful tiding
Eternity for lives abiding.

As Jesus spoke—a diadem
With Holy words remained.

So pray all men and say amen
For love be not restrained.

ooooo

Unpredictable Times

How unpredictable the times are. We think we are set for awhile and some new disaster and/or tragedy comes up. We journalists learn to stay with the status quo. Between the time I compose this and two weeks we may be the United States of Something Else. Who knows? By the time you read this I will, hopefully, be home from my holidays in Atlanta spent with Pat and family there. Christmas here was my gift exchange with sons, Dave and Harry, and families. Dave is a fishing guide in Shasta and wife Jan is with the Department of Social Services. Both are avid fishing advocates. Harry and Lillian and their daughters, Emily, 14, and Ashley, 10, came in from Willits.

Music Recital

David Burnett's workshop recital was performing here in time to catch the first rains. In order to accommodate all of his pupils and parents, it was the second of two recitals.

At the piano were Darius Wadia, Elma Ackley, Lisa Fanthorpe White, Hilary Walters, Brian Johnson, Jessica Johnson, Jamie Balfe, Vera Hicks, Danielle Mercury, Elizabeth Brusati, and Renee Ward. Each rendered several selections. The program ended with the delightful soprano solo, "O Holy Night," by Erin Hurley, accompanied on the flute by Renee Ward and at the piano by Mr. Burnett.

Students and guests assembled in the fire-lit drawing room of the Burnett home on San Francisco Boulevard to hear all the lovely Christmas carols presented by the children.

When ready to leave, the heavens had opened with our first real shower in months.

David and wife, Dana, are also deeply involved with horses out in Sleepy Hollow and have their own stock corrals in Woodacre.

Rich Hausen, a former local boy, was seen on TV recently by his friends as he was going out to the Persian Gulf to serve in Operation Desert Shield.

The son of the late Wayne and Terry Ellerman, Rick attended San Anselmo schools before going to Vietnam where he served in the Green Berets. Later he was employed in the state hospital and prison systems for a number of years before joining the Novato Fire Department. The Ellermans for years operated the Tiny Tot Photography Studio on Tunstead Avenue here. They were active business people and both avid fishermen. Following her demise, Wayne, who was a music major at college, joined a traveling music group that became popular in Mendocino County. Friends later learned that he, too, had passed on.

Rick's folks' business and housing were located across the street from San Anselmo's fire house then. The loud sirens and excitement of the rolling engines no doubt influenced the lad in determining his like of work and possibly his life in the service of his country.

My plane just landed last night and I find my pipes had burst in the backyard and left icicles on my clothesline and chunks of ice on the patio. Neighbors had kindly had the water turned off at the sidewalk, and Clare was feeding my cats, so 18-year-old Mai Tai and 18-month-old Missy are doing fine, thank you. Jackie and Toby, the two shitzus, are happily at the groomers where they get special care.

ooooo

History Repeats

"This is the time when all good men come to the aid of their country." How many times have typing students executed this statement in their keyboard practice skills? The old war slogan "A slip of the lip can sink a ship" slips back in war days. A sign of stability is to trust our God and leaders regardless of deleterious wordage that insults us all. Faith gives an inner solidarity to see us through the stress of war.

History does repeat itself and a brief but resolute meeting of San Anselmo's Historical Commission recently emphasized creating a society or auxiliary to the commission. The meeting Wednesday, presided over by Thomas Perry in absence of Katharine Coddington, was a discussion mainly of the advisability of reaching out to meet and include more of the town's old-timers. On the committee to implement this are Sherry DeVaux and Laurie Smith.

Pat Swensen enlarged on the success of the annual dinner at the local Seminary and a vote approved it to be held there this year. Mrs. Swensen stated that she had sent a letter to the owner of a pioneer home asking if he would allow it to be used in a house tour later this spring for historical purposes.

An increase in visitors' interest in the museum under the library has been noticed and Mr. Perry offered to assist in coordinating museum visiting with visibility in the San Anselmo Library, aiding Barbara Jacobs, town librarian.

Bill Franchini's financial report was encouraging with additional funds realized in various projects.

Old Media

Randy Thompson owns the Packaging Store at San Anselmo's hub corner (Miracle Mile) and has a deep love of this community and Marin. Randy's father was the late Bill Thompson, for years manager of Marin's radio station KITM some 20 years ago. His co-workers, the erstwhile Kitty Oppenheimer, gave her voice many years to the local airways. Known as a founder of the Ross Valley Players and the Marin Music Chest, Kitty was the most widely known person hereabouts. Randy recalls his own experience in the media when he wrote a commercial for Northwestern Savings to run with the Kiddies' Voices.

He resides with his sister Cindy and a very active brother-in-law, Derek, in Fairfax. The latter has Derek's Pool Service and has a band called Next in which he plays guitar. Randy is also a musician, but his hobby is exotic fish which are maintained in a large home tank.

Lend an Ear

Many have personal tragedies already and the war crisis has made these almost unbearable. Your phone calls now will usually entail some kindly counseling, so count it a plus if you are able to give a kind listening ear to someone. This is when it's needed the most.

Poet for the Community

Stefanie Marlis came to San Francisco in 1973 from Buffalo, New York to spend the winter. She never left and now resides here in San Anselmo.

Award winning poet, college teacher and consultant with artists, she soon found her place in the community. With a master's degree in creative writing from San Francisco State University, she came here in 1975 with her partner, Eliot Holtzman, portrait photographer of San Rafael, writing his brochures and aiding his business. After they split, she continued on writing her poetry.

Her first award was the prestigious Joseph Henry Jackson Award (named for the literary editor of the *San Francisco Chronicle*) and the Marin Arts Council Grant with her first book *Red Tools* in 1984. The Marin Poetry Center was instigated by her and Peter Sharkey in 1981 at Falkirk in San Rafael, giving poets a meeting center.

Slow Joy her second book, won the Brittingham Prize at the University of Wisconsin for best 50-page manuscript. Last year she gave her poetry readings at the two campuses of the University of Wisconsin. Her latest prize is a tour of poetry reading at 12 colleges in the midwest in April. This is a writer's award from the Great Lakes College Association which also pays for the readings. San Anselmo will be privileged to hear these readings here at Oliver's Book Store on San Anselmo on February 15 at 8 pm.

Stefanie is one busy young lady as she teaches a class of 25 at College of Marin and a smaller group at her home twice a week. If that weren't enough, she has the Stefanie Marlis Advertising company, now six months old with clients and services that don't hurt people or the earth. Her clients include Terry Pierce, management consultant of "Inside Impact," Los Camillos, a Mexican food restaurant in San Rafael, and "Perfect Health Joy Songs" at Larkspur Landing.

Stefanie's first poetry prize won at the age of 11 in Eden, New York was a chocolate Easter rabbit.

McClure's Beach
Above the sunset-washed cliffs
covered with graffiti
the size Jupiter might have lettered
as proof to Juno, the gold sea-life made coins
of the undersides of air-borne headland birds.
Later in your room the jazz
by a musician I had forgotten
(I recognized the clarity, the verve)
unheard since on another coast, years ago,
love's small fires proved as inexhaustible.

—Stefanie Marlis

ooooo

A view of the Jonathan Kittle home and estate in 1870 in Ross. This is currently the grounds of the Marin Art and Garden Center with its many public functions. Roy Farrington Jones Private Collection.

History in the Making

Yellow ribbons are out of stock in most stores as citizens are paying their own heartfelt tribute to the military in the Persian Gulf. Many homes have anti-war declarations although sympathetic to our youth over there. Also individual homes have gone all out with ribbons and flags; trees here and there (like on the Miracle Mile) have the statements made with gigantic ribbons and bows, reminding all what's on the hearts of everyone.

"Lord, may the desert storm pass quickly" is a placard prayer designed by St. Anselm's Church here for its parishioners to be a reminder of those serving in the Gulf War.

According to Pat Langley, coordinator of the 1100 family church, those in the mideast war are listed there and in the church bulletin.

They are: STC Martin De La Torrie, Captain Mark Powell, Ted Bennett, Captain Rick Bonner, Captain C. Mead, Captain Rose Mead, Private First Class Michael Rinaldi, Major Tony Gilmore, Christ Machi, Brian Oswald, Quincy Cassidy, Robert Herdzik, Ken R. White, John Brennan, Lieutenant Junior Grade Raymond Grechman, Dr. Francis Parnell, Matthew Theomes, First Sergeant Anthony Bricca, Sergeant Mike A. Rohe, and Captain Celeste McInerney.

Plans are being made to have the prayer placed on buttons and bumper stickers.

A Cultural Memorial

Mrs. Norman Livermore of Ross was responsible for purchase of the land from the Jonathan Kittles, which now houses the Marin Art and Garden Center, back in 1943.

She united eight autonomous groups to form a non-profit which handled the sale for $25,000, payable within five years. When the

Kittles decided to sell back in 1943, Mrs. Livermore, a visionary and president of the Marin Conservation League, considered the land to be of great beauty with its beautiful gardens and trees as a living memorial. And it has become just that being dedicated to the cultural and natural assets of Marin with a growing community within its boundaries to ascertain this be continued.

This was part of the Mexican land grant called "Rancho Punto de Quentin." James Ross, for whom the town was named, had settled there in 1859 on the west side of San Anselmo Creek, which was known as Ross Landing. They built their home on a portion of the property, and George Worn, who married Ross's daughter, planted a small magnolia tree in the center. This has grown to such proportions and beauty as to attract worldwide recognition.

The Ross's home, known as "Sunnyside" was sold to the Kittle family, who remodeled it. The house was later torn down due to a roof fire. Remaining are the Barn, now used by the Ross Valley Players and the familiar Octagon house.

The Center now has six founder groups and six affiliate groups. It was declared a Living Memorial in memory of those who sacrificed their lives while in the service of their country.

Serving as current president of the center is Mrs. William Davis, a daughter of another pioneer, the late Judge Frederick Crisp, San Anselmo's magistrate.

ooooo

Keeping Equilibrium

How does one keep his equilibrium these days what with war, drought, depression and recession? No matter what, you can't avoid the news (as chilling as it is on CNN) because as citizens we have to be informed, as water users we must know the limits and we have to know money conservation too.

Personal Peace Actions

Discover the particular strength you can bring to the emergency we're facing. Create a poster, poem, button, chain letter, counseling service, fund raising event, fast, etc. Take strong steps toward a sustainable lifestyle. Transform our excessive dependency on oil. Bicycle, walk, conserve, recycle, garden. Build community close to home. Breathe deeply when you notice you are feeling isolated, helpless, confused, in grief. Take time to center and nurture yourself.

The above is from an anonymous card passed around to the public that is feeling depression or qualms about what is going on in the Mid-east. It encourages support of our troops while suggesting personal things to relieve tensions.

Armageddon?

Betty Kenner, manager of the Christian General Store, located on San Anselmo's Miracle Mile (part of Fourth Street), says that Hal Lindsay books, i.e., *The Late Great Planet Earth*, and others are sold out, and it is difficult keeping stock in about Armageddon and the end times. Noted theologians interviewed on TV state the subject was largely ignored until the Mid-east conflagrations began. Then it was realized that it was prophecy (from the Bible) coming true and that those wars were declared to be the beginning of the end times. Men of the cloth will declare that Heaven only knows and just stay close to your God.

Our Troops

Ken and Ruby White, San Anselmans, have a personal interest in the Gulf War as their son, St. Sgt. Allan White is stationed there with the U.S. Air Force. He was located in Germany after seven years of service and sent to the Gulf when war broke out. Allan has been a mechanic and can now pilot planes so his talents are useful. He graduated from the local schools and Sir Francis Drake High School. A cousin, Mrs. White's nephew from Petaluma, is also seeing service over there.

From Fairfax Jacqueline Water's son, Sgt. Aaron Leonard, also a local high school grad, is serving as a Ground Surveillance Systems Operator in the Mid-east. Leonard was involved with the Drake music bands and was a member of DeMolay. His wife, Kimberly, is a student at Kansas State University.

A Redwood High graduate, Capt. Louise Reeves flies a refueling tanker plane in the Gulf war. She is an aerospace engineering grad from University of Colorado at Boulder. On January 12 she returned there for a second duty tour overseas.

❧

They were stomping the boards at the old Kittle barn Saturday for the Ross Valley Players' production of *The Mystery of Edwin Drood* on the site of the Marin Art and Garden Center.

Currently the John Brebners are hoping to raise more funds to make improvements on the playhouse as more storage is needed for set assemblies, etc. The super-drama about Edwin Drood was one of their best and continues on next weekend. The lively audience, encourage to participate in the gala play, ended it all with shouts of "Bravo."

We remember the main publicist for the Players in the early days who was the late Kitty Oppenheimer of Ross. She was eventually put in charge of a newsy Marin radio program, thus ending her days happily. So much has been done by early individualists who set the stage for later successes.

Closing Up Shop

Lee Morris, operator of Ross Valley Stationers here, doesn't want to give up his nine-year business but is forced into it. Owner of the building, Thomas Rig, now wants to occupy it with production of his real estate magazine. Next door Mack Photo was compelled to close its doors at Christmas, creating the absence of a fine art photographer in the person of Ruth Williamsen of Fairfax.

The stationer's wife, Peggy, worked there on Fridays and by March 1 the shop closes down, interrupting a fine, longtime relationship with patronage, who enjoyed its proximity to the post office. Lee's personality was exceptional in his rapport with people and his customers regret his departure.

The couple plan on travel in a motorhome to Washington D.C. and vicinity to see the sights. Before coming here he was a car salesman in Novato.

Local Protester

Did you know that Elizabeth Kent, wife of Congressman William Kent of the town that bears their name was a protester at one time? Yes, she marched in Washington for women's suffrage and was even incarcerated for a time (briefly, we record). Mrs. Kent was one of the area's finest ladies and leaders and worked with her husband in the preservation of so many of our historical sights.

Also D. Frank Monte, former mayor of San Anselmo, was one of the biggest sellers of war bonds in the second World War. Many a rally was held at the San Anselmo Tamalpais Theater with Frank, the inimitable M.C. presiding on the stage. Actor, singer, he was never without words and was an impresario par excellence.

The Pajama Game

The *Pajama Game*, done by dazzling professionals, was truly a great performance as one of a series of great performances for 1991 at a packed Angelica Hall for public benefit Thursday.

A great many seniors of the area have selected these plays and well they have, due to the up-beat nature of the shows.

Guest stars included Sandra Simpson, Jeff Bodnar, Paul Kerr, Janice Madden, and Ken Andrews, and they all have also had starring roles in *West Side Story*, *Fiddler on the Roof*, *The Rainmaker*, *Gypsy*, *Sweet Charity* and other leading national hits.

By March the Veterans' Auditorium will be completely refurbished and available for the Kingston Trio and Ferrante, leading pianist.

ooooo

The Land We Live In

The good news ... sounds on my San Anselmo skylight on Wednesday at 5 am told me it was so. The long-awaited rainfall was entering. With great glee I arose and ran into the yard to join in the pitter-patter, bucket the rain spouts, all the while reveling in God's goodness to us.

I had long prepared for the drought onslaught with a no-no on the water faucets and any planting. However, there came a ray of hope as the dampness and misty drops enveloped me. We complain but miss it so much when the great lever in the sky is turned off. Woe is us then.

At the same time the war ended and our youth will be coming home. Will the winner raise his hand—the good old USA or Uncle Sam is once more victorious over the enemy. Yes, it's all over but the shouting—Iraq and Saddam Hussein have had it.

The rain lack has sent birds into our yards. A two-year-old eagle, seen in the Barber tract, a black swan walking the Seminary grounds, and my small bird bath being deluged with sparrows unable to wait their turn. Tom Perry of Sunnyside Nursery fame has had a barrage of press people curious as to how he'll handle the rain lack. The Perrys are pioneers of San Anselmo, being related to the Worn and Ross families (originators of Ross).

One of our going volunteer concerns is the Thrift Shop conducted by the Auxiliary of the Marin Humane Society in San Anselmo. Coming March 15 they will be celebrating their 30 years in one place with a party at the local shop. They have supported the spay and neuter clinic of the Society of particular aid to pet owners. Mary Ball says that hundreds of volunteers have happily served the public with purchases to enhance the cause of animals.

I did promise more names of local youth serving in the Persian

Gulf War. Representing the U.S. Army are Robert Lewis, Josh Joslin and Jeff Blank of San Anselmo and Wes Easley and Mike Purvis of San Rafael. Further info must be obtained from families.

Oldies but Goodies

Remember the days of Bill and Ada Fusselman? He was San Anselmo mayor and a Marin supervisor and her name is still synonymous with College of Marin. The library on the Kentfield campus was named for her as she served on the college board for 33 years (non-salaried).

She and Bill were married in Washington state, leaving an impressive line of credentials behind them to settle in San Anselmo. They opened their first restaurant and candy store here, making a name for themselves in this as well as dispensing their personality and charm for which they later became well-known in Marin.

On their 50th wedding anniversary in 1964, Ada, who was first a wife and homemaker received this accolade in the form of a poem; "What's her line. Self-employed dealer in service to all of Marin. Artist in pastry and candy making, singer, comedienne, sparking MC, always cheerful and life of the party, book reviewer, popular current event speaker, a leader in war time and peace, educator. All who knew her say, 'Thank you, Ada, for all you have done for us and our County.'"

When her husband Bill became a nay-sayer about the building of the Marin Civic Center, she was supportive of his ability to have the courage of his convictions.

Their names stand as an impressive influence for the area's good citizens and those to follow. Educators, mayor, supervisors, noted public speakers—a hard line to follow.

ooooo

Winter Storm

Since last August the world has been on a roller coaster ride and the variable times are hardly believable.

In our fifth drought year, we declared a war on Iraq, thousands of our youth were shipped to the Persian Gulf. In a few months we won the war. Tears were scarcely dried over their departure when they were home and the weeping was for gladness. Water rationing began and with it came rain storms of great magnitude, from Desert Storm to winter storm. So we say, now what?

Perhaps Ecclesiastes 3 can say it better:
> There is a time for everything;
> A time to be born;
> A time to die ...

The deaths from the war are cause for much national grief. Healing begins now with time and consolation of the merciful.

Our munitions pouring onto the lands of the Arabian desert have provoked a destruction that Americans are going to help repair.

A time to grieve for those in the military who lost their lives while in the service of their country.

A Time to Be Quiet ... A Time to Speak Up
Walter Matthau walked out of a local bakery after hearing the price of a cake was $27.50. He was enacting his role in an upcoming TV movie "Running Out" to be shown May 12 on CBS. Charles Matthau, his son, is the director. Lexi Ashton was the counter girl. The story involves a young orphaned boy whose sole support is an ailing grandmother. Matthau becomes the hero as he steps in to help the boy and takes over at the end.

A Time to Find

Marin Cancer Society's Discovery Shop was the recipient of some treasures in the form of holiday miniatures and unique crafts donated by an exclusive shop that needed space for new articles.

Rushed into service for display of the articles through March were local volunteers Marie Gallagher, Mary Lou Flynn, and Jean Vaccaro of Fairfax; Barbara Shindelus of San Anselmo; Clarissa Gillis, of Kentfield; Jean McCabe of Corte Madera; Nadine Hewitt of Lucas Valley; and Helen Bayer and Marian Pilotte of Novato.

A Time to Plant

In spite of the increased rainfall, growers are expected to be in trouble anyway. The grounds are benefitting but rise in water storage hasn't caught up.

A Time to Speak Up

The mostly grey-haired audience sat in silence to hear and watch an extravaganza of talent and sound at Angelica Hall last week. The Three Lamplighters, widely acclaimed musical entertainers in country music, were preceded by William Ferrante, noted piano artist. The silence ended with immense applause.

A Time to Dance

Our own Chuck Lavaroni and his Swing Society band played the Irish tunes for the Marin Solo's St. Patrick's dance Saturday at the San Anselmo Recreation Hall.

A time for loving—the dance group has had several romances blossoming among the members. Lew Bortfeld and his bride, the former Alice Thompson, have just returned from a South Pacific honeymoon. As former club officers, they received flowers and danced the anniversary waltz. Lew is also a soloist with the band. Another couple, Ed and Maddie Dennim of San Anselmo, were married March 17, 1990, and received ovations.

Memory of the Irish
If you've ever been born Irish
Then you know just what I mean.

Your fancy turns into a dish
Just fit for a queen.

You're happy even if you mourn
for sad times seldom stay.

Your heart may be so badly torn
But doesn't stay that way.

For optimists these Irish are
Born in a land so green.

And generations hold the star
They sing when times are mean.

So if you've known an Irishman
With manner that's carefree

It's because he's touched by God's hand
To cheer up you and me.

—Larine O'Brien Brown
March 17, 1984

ooooo

A view of main street (now Sir Francis Drake Boulevard) taken in 1908. To the left is the train depot and in the background is Red Hill. The town of San Anselmo was then called the "Junction." Roy Farrington Jones Private Library.

Pictures of San Anselmo

Pictures of how San Anselmo looked in the days of horse-and-buggy and how quaint it was before the automobile. Many old-timers can remember these times and would enjoy the display now awaiting their visit at the San Anselmo Public Library on Tunstead Avenue here.

Among them are the "San Anselmo Junction," circa 1875, as the local town was then named, looking toward Ross with a horse drawn cart at the station; Mrs. William Wesell shown in a horse drawn buggy (1900); the Deysher and Lafargue Garage and Blacksmith Shop (1900-1910); the foreground of San Francisco Theological Seminary (1890-1900); the horse drawn fire wagon, prior to 1917 with the fire horses named "Major" and "Colonel"; a horse drawn surrey with a fringe on top used by the Frank Howard Allen family when they lived at 165 Crescent Road here; a dual horse powered surrey parked in front of the livery stable (1900); horse wagons do the heavy work at the E.K. Wood Lumber Yard (where Bayview Savings now stands) 1900-1920; the old Hub depot, backed by Red Hill, has a train in and a waiting horse-pulled cart; the Clute family children ride in a pony cart (1907); the July 4th parade of 1909 had many cameras out and pictured were a decorated flatbed containing costumed young girls, the "Grande Dame" on a fanciful flower bedecked horse drawn cart, ladies riding singly in white gowns on horses—a herd of fillies; a large decorated wagon carrying children, and local firemen with their decorated firewagon.

Barbara Jacobs, the town librarian, was responsible for the historical photo display. She is also a member of the San Anselmo Historical Commission.

Emma White's Birthday

Emma Segale White's life of 80 years was honored Saturday with a large reception at the St. Anselm's Recreation Hall.

The San Anselmo pioneer has for the past 50 years lived in her home on Medway Avenue here where she raised her two boys, Paul and Dennis, who are now six foot men.

Her granddaughter, Debbie White of Klamath Falls, Oregon, a university student, assisted her grandmother in cutting the cake. She also presented her grandma with a plaque of a handmade and embroidered angel and poem. Mrs. White collects angels.

Friends came from Oregon, Southern California, the peninsula, East Bay, Eureka, Sacramento and Napa as well as North Beach in San Francisco where Mrs. White was born and raised. Her folks came from Genoa, Italy, and she was raised in all the fine cooking traditions of that area. This writer's mouth was watering as she spoke of her home-made ravioli (which she gives to friends!). Her North Beach chums Helen and Al Minetti who were in her wedding party came over for the event.

Emma (now we're on a first name basis) tells me that Genoa is noted for its basil pesto recipe, made with garlic, olive oil and cheese. Meals are always prepared with home-grown items and homemade. She raised her children alone, so to speak, but did a bang-up job with a welcome mat open for all. Summers then were spent picnicking with the neighbors at Taylor Park, McNears, or China Camp. There was spontaneous fun with unplanned trips which made for wonderful lives. Singing and music played a great part as the family is talented.

The local matriarch is very happy in her job as assistant coordinator of noon meals at Whistlestop where she has been for ten years. She adores working around people including the many refugees in Marin. She walks to church, St. Rita's in Fairfax, as it's closer and she is an active member of Italian Catholic Federation No. 16 of Fairfax.

ooooo

Postcard from the South

The Old South with its dogwood bloom springs and its heavy anti-bellum social customs of charm and hospitality still remains regardless of infiltration from everywhere.

The songs and a simple happiness that outlive the Civil War can be felt with a smile and a handshake. Done with the ease of generations, the simplest folk with a few droll words can break down the coolest reserve.

However, they retain their heritage and pride, and won't give an inch on the Civil War, the one that cost more lives than all our wars combined. Vestiges of the old South are seen beside the roads in plaques commemorating battle scenes. Here and there among the condos some have retained their old farms, living in houses dating back to the war. Like a postcard from history they retain nostalgic memories.

Cars rush by and exhaust fills the air. There are miles of trees (where the blue-coats marched). Will they be cut for condos in years to come? Will they be gone with the wind? The daily *Atlanta Constitution* is obviously not being dictated to and tells the stories in truth.

A short drive east of Atlanta lies the picturesque towns of ante-bellum Georgia. In Milledgville the old Governor's Mansion is an exquisite example of Greek Revival architecture; Washington (founded during the Revolutionary War); Athens (home of the oldest state university) and Madison, a treasure of antibellum buildings.

It was 14 years ago that daughter Pat, husband John, and their four redheads moved back there. With my late husband, Charles, we made biannual trips back and as I continue, it has become my home away from home. Their three-story home in the Rivergate section of Dunwoody was designed by Pat and is a charmer. The two older boys, Ron and Rich, are on their own now, and there are two teenagers left, John, 17 and Shana, 14, in high school. The house will undoubtedly be changed for a smaller one some day, but the memories linger on …

Generational Business

David Baxus who is a new antique dealer in town had about four generations here before him in San Anselmo.

The young man has bought out the Witherspoon and Postlewait Antiques in the old Tamalpais Theater building at 332 Sir Francis Drake Boulevard here. He had previously had an antique store outlet in San Rafael.

The son of Mr. and Mrs. Andrew Baxus of Mill Valley, the young man graduated from Old Mill and Edna Maguire School and Tamalpais High School, as well as Anthony's Real Estate in Terra Linda. The store here will feature unusual items and pieces from estate buying.

David is the grand-nephew of the late Arthur and Clara Shearer of San Anselmo. The Shearer plumbing business on Tunstead Avenue was a leading one in its day. His mother's grandparents, the Vonderheides conducted a delicatessen in Lansdale many years ago.

⊷⊶

The Reverend Herb Ireland of Sparks, Nevada was visiting his mother, Mrs. Bill Ireland here this week With his wife Caroline and sister Sherry Angeloni, of Novato, the trio boarded a plane for Maui, Hawaii, where he will fill the pulpit at the Nazarene church there for two weeks.

The young man is a product of San Anselmo schools and entered the Pasadena Nazarene Seminary at the age of 17. In Nevada he has been president of the ministerial association.

Compassionate Volunteer

I'm going to tell you about a lady, Helen, pioneer of San Anselmo who volunteers all of her free time to care for the aged in a local nursing home. Her devotion began when her 90-year-old mother was in need of nursing home care. In went Helen to feed her mom three times daily and oversee her care.

Even after her mother passed on, Helen kept on coming because she had formed an attachment for others in the home. They need that extra ray of hope that Helen gives them. Now she's on full time volunteering. She's just happy giving of her time and talents to these elderly, oft times desperately ill and lonely people.

Helen had always wanted to be a nurse, so she loves to do it. Never is self-acclaim mentioned, and she doesn't want it. That would spoil it for her, but we just wanted you to know we still have genuine people around. Their names aren't out in front, but we know who they are. Bless them.

ooooo

The Albert Dibblee home in Ross in the 1870's. It later become the Katharine Branson School for girls. Roy Farrington Jones Private Library.

Intriguing Families

Some of the families who found their place here in the Ross Valley and seldom departed from it are the ones I've found intriguing. Many of them were people of means and many were not, but whatever the case, they loved this scenic area. Oh, how they love it now! It's not only a heavenly spot, but Caesar is in it, too.

Four of Ross's oldest families had one forebear in common, as well as his wife. He was Lucius Hamilton Allen, who was born in Potsdam, New York in 1817. He was married in the early 1840's to Sarah DeWitt and in 1851 moved to San Francisco to engage in "mercantile pursuits." His wife and four children joined in 1858.

A Century Ago

General and Mrs. Allen (who died in 1887 and 1888, respectively) had four children. Son Henry married Fanny Wyatt and built a home at the end of Allen Avenue in Ross that was later known as the J.K. Armsby estate and home. In 1865 daughter Harriet married Jonathan Kittle, who was 20 years her senior. After a stay in New York they bought the estate of the Worn family on Lagunitas Road in Ross that was called "Sunnyside." To accommodate their family of four children they had the size of the house doubled by remodeling. Today this estate with its "octagon" house and stable (now known as The Barn) is the Marin Art and Garden Center, known so widely as a public cultural center where all are encouraged to come. Their daughter, Isabel Kittle, married Benjamin H. Dibblee in 1905. He was one of four children of Albert Dibblee whose family lived at Fernhill, now the site of the Katharine Branson School.

The Allen's fourth child, Sally, married James Coffin in 1878. They often visited her sister and family the Kittles in Ross. Later they built a home on Shady Lane there.

The Coffin's eldest daughter, Marion, married John Shepherd Eels and they had three children. Their second daughter, Natalie, married A. Crawford Greene and their five children are James Coffin Greene, of Pasadena, Anne Stine, Natalie G. Lewis, A. Crawford Greene, Jr., and Sheila G. Peck.

'82 Flood

Over a thousand San Anselmans relived the '82 flood Saturday by viewing the movie at Bayview Federal Bank here. The film was taken at the flood scene by Ben Burtt, then a cinematographer employed by Lucas Films at 321 San Anselmo Avenue at the time.

Theresa Stawowy, coordinator of the San Anselmo Volunteer Effort, introduced Mr. Burtt and described the happenings of the day. She was assisted by Debbie Stutsman of SAVE and Carol Roe, the bank manager, who served coffee. A Chinese chicken salad was donated by Glenn Miwa of Comfort's restaurant.

Beginning at 9:30 a.m., the film was shown on a large screen nine times for thirty minute periods. Appropriate music and wording was dubbed in, including Winston Churchill's war time speech.

Those attending were given paper to write out their most interesting experience in the flood. All of Ross Valley was inundated with overflowing creeks, and hillside houses fell.

Ken and Mary Ellen Ball had many experiences, including watching Mozart Kaufman carrying a woman on his back from his store just before the wooden bridge fell. He slipped once, but hurriedly rescued her.

My husband Charles, inspector at Fairfax, had problems doubled when angry citizens came into Fairfax Town Hall threatening civil suit. The secretaries there were overwhelmed and needed an experienced hand there. Charles was a retiree of state construction where he was a senior inspector.

ooooo

Reversals of Weather

Reversals of weather have been mystifying. It used to be March winds and April showers bring May flowers. Mother Nature has had her months mixed up, but, regardless, the flowers are beautiful. No one promised us a rose garden either, but they are all in bloom; old-fashioned climbers, velvety red, short bloom yellow and the tea rose, all planted through many years. Do roses mean love and reminiscences of other days? Garden lovers lived here. Since 1906? The Browns left part of themselves in the growing plants.

Friends said to write about my recent "indisposition." I can only say that for a week I was "out of it." My neck stiffened so that I couldn't move it. From Sunday until Friday I was phoning the medics and telling them to send an ambulance. Some nurse would say sweetly, "Just give it time and rest!" She was most convincing. Following many medical facility visits and six bottles of pills, I realized she was correct after all. Pain doesn't want to listen to reason. The cause? Lifting buckets of water. Son, the realist, said, "Mom, water is cheaper than doctors." Some people learn the hard way.

Library Place

There is an alley they call Library Place that runs from Magnolia Street, back of the San Anselmo Police Department, the historical museum, and the public library onto Tunstead Avenue. This seems to have been a central place around which my life in San Anselmo revolved. As a school girl in Ross I would come into the *San Anselmo Herald* office on Tunstead after school to visit mom, who was Agnes O'Brien, editor. I would sit on a stool with pencil in hand, writing anything waiting for mom. Next door on Library Place was Shearer's Plumbing—Arthur and Clara Shearer and daughter, Helen, lived upstairs. Helen and I became fast friends and commuted daily on the Tam special for Tamalpais High.

Later after college I entered journalism on the old weekly *Marin Journal*, oldest paper in California, in San Rafael. Then I met and married Charles H. Brown, a San Anselmo native. His mother, Kate, spotted a house at the end of Tunstead Avenue. We bought it and our family was raised there—all near Library Place. Daughter Pat was the reader and covered most books in the children's division of the Carnegie Library at Library Place. Charles, volunteer fireman, would cut through Library Place in his haste to reach the firehouse for the first engine departure.

Now I return to the scene of my childhood as I attend meetings of the San Anselmo Historical Commission in the museum ... at Library Place. Our nephew, Charles Monte, director of Chapel of the Hills, finds it very familiar, too, as he serves on the Commission meeting in the museum with the old family scenes of yesteryear.

Rosie's Entry

Although a teacher and professional floral arranger, Rosie Echelmeier had never entered a floral competition. When she did in the first annual Larkspur Flower and Food Show recently in Escalle, she was a "best of show" winner in the master division for friendship gardens.

Her exquisite entry was unusual in that it had two sections connected by a twig bridge and mood moss. The elevated twig structure was covered with mood moss and built on twig basket shapes. Among the manzanita twigs rising up from this were satellite floral arrangements. Colors were in lavender, burgundy and pink. Roses were freeze dried and looked fresh and original.

Rosie's Flower Market on Tunstead Avenue here is something to see and she gives classes for adults and children in arrangements. Two of her employees, Cristina Blomberg and Caroline Klenk of Forest Knolls, were also prize winners. The former won first master's division for elegant table arrangement. The latter won second for her floral arrangement in the master division. The Market number is 456-6862.

Red Hill

Red Hill—under its presence motorists drive to and from neighboring cities at the Hub arterial signs. It's that big patch of red earth located near the Red Hill Shopping Center.

It has been much talked about through the years. Way back before the turn of the century, Dr. Henry DuBois owned it as well as the Tamalpais Cemetery (at the end of San Rafael's Fifth Street). He decided to build a road over the hill with cheap labor. Too late he discovered that horse-and-buggy couldn't make it to the top! The humor of the situation, in which a doctor would own a cemetery, caught on with Corte Madera's Frank Pixley, editor of the *San Francisco Argonaut*. He continually lampooned the local medic on the subject.

Again the hill was in the news in 1967. A massive slide occurred, creating a $300,000 loss when four apartment buildings being built there collapsed.

ooooo

Frederick Crisp Home. San Anselmo Historical Commission.

Genuine People

There must have been 100 of us on the Senior bus tour of Sacramento last week. It was just after Rail Fair '91 and a hot Jazz Festival coming up on the weekend. Sacto was climbing into the '90's weather-wise.

We had a fun-packed two days there with shopping in Old Town, lunch aboard the Delta King, a tour of the huge Diamond Almond plant. A movie showed that California is the world's almond capital. The almond is also a terrific nut, flavorful and delicious. The next day was our tour of the beautiful State Capitol building and grounds where history is uppermost. A guide described the historical meanings of the 100-year-old structure, of how its prime facets were hidden until reconstruction brought out many jewels of California's historical years. The grounds are kept as they were, lawns, hedges, very old and tall trees and an abundance of friendly squirrels.

My own grandma was a California native as were her parents down in San Diego back in 1860, so it's easy to relate history in buildings and in the life-styles current then.

The Commission

San Anselmo's Historical Commission met last week and is hot on the trail of old homes. Much discussion was held on researching same with the intent of conducting a series of historical town walks, similar to those conducted ten years ago.

Names of pioneer residences such as Morgan, Wright, Carrigan, Taylor and Bugbee as well as many surrounding the Seminary were suggested as possible visiting sites.

Replacing Katherine Coddington, of Ross, who resigned her chair, are the co-chairwomen, Laurie Smith and Karen Libertore. Pat Swenson was appointed secretary. There is to be a training program for volunteers working at the Historical Museum, and Barbara Jacobs, town librarian, was asked to check out an expenditure. Bill Franchini presented his financial report, followed by discussion on proper storage, filing and building data discs, led by Chuck Swensen.

The annual dinner sponsored by the Commission is to be held on October 16 at the Seminary, according to Pat Swensen, the chairwoman. The following week will be their historical homes tour of the Seminary area. The century-old San Francisco Presbyterian Theological Seminary has many beautiful home landmarks, some inhabited by the professors and their families through the years. The landscape design of the area is also a distinguished one. The public will be invited to attend these events.

Naming of Greenfield

Back in 1930 the San Anselmo City Council ordered the paving of a popular street and inquired of Monash Greenfield if they could name the street for him. Monash, a native of Russia and former San Franciscan, had the Greenfield Candy Factory which hadn't been too lucrative, but welcomed the honor of having a street named after him. His former home on Maple Avenue in Kentfield across from the college still stands. His son and wife, Jacob and Hannah Greenfield, resided in San Anselmo, and Hannah became a longtime employee of Ward's, Albert's and Macy's in San Rafael. She died in 1978. Two granddaughters remain here, Esther Goldbaum of San Anselmo and Doreen Glicksberg of Kentfield. Then there's a great-granddaughter and husband, Janis and Cesar Hernandes, San Francisco schoolteachers who live on Meadowcroft Avenue here and have a young son, Samuel, a student at the Marin Primary School.

Doreen and Esther attended Wade Thomas School and Tamalpais High School and enjoy harkening back to the days when Valerie Ansel was the grammar school principal and how they loved her as a person. Miss Ansel was an institution in herself and students graduating from her eighth grade were the highest scholastic freshmen.

The Day the Rationing Began
March 1, 1991

This is the day the district said
We are rationing from the shed.

You can have 50 gallons per
to wash your skin and your pet's fur.

Don't forget big brother's looking
In your pot as you are cooking.

Keep your faucets extra tight
Help prevent Marin's big blight.

You can do it if you try
This is no time to be shy.

If you see some neighbor that
Hurries past you with a vat.

Or leaves the hose running while
Responding to a neighbor's smile.

Report same to MMWD
Preserve us from iniquity.

ooooo

A shuttle train of the Northwestern Pacific Rail Road makes the trip from San Anselmo to Fairfax in 1940. Jack Farley Collection.

The Farleys

Neighbors can form ties as rewarding as families, especially in these days when moving is common.

So it was with the Farleys and O'Briens who lived out on Fifth Street in San Rafael during the '30's. John C. Farley had been a WWI veteran and returned to marry Alice Dufaus, the lovely daughter of the Jean Dufaus, French laundry people there. Their little son John Anthony (Jack), was raised in the French Catholic tradition at St. Raphael's and attended St. Anselm's School.

Moving in next door was a widow, Mrs. Agnes A. O'Brien and three children, Patricia, John and Larine (me) and later our grandma, Mrs. John A. O'Brien.

Through the years, the families formed close relationships. Grandma Dufaus' delicious homemade soup was often passed to our house. Little Jack came over to play with our dog, Bonzo, as his cat was elderly. The grandmothers, alone during the day, could gossip out back and spoil the dog with endless cookies. The mothers had mutual respect as both were professionals. Alice Farley had taught school out in Tiburon and Agnes was an editor on the *Marin Journal*.

Alice, the teacher, inspired us as we studied and watched over us during my mother's absence. In 1935 my mother was stricken at her desk on the *Journal* and passed on three weeks later. The Howard MacKenzies taught me journalism and hired me. He had been a printer on the *New York Times*. I learned by doing.

Meanwhile, Pat married Peter Durel and later became a social worker. John served four years overseas in WWII in active combat. He later became a rancher in Williams, Ca. The Farleys remained as supportive friends as we went on with our lives and had children. Young Jack even then was fascinated by our railroad system in this county.

Even as I speak, Jack Farley, now a senior, has become a walking vocal history of the Northwestern Pacific Railroad in this county and all over the state. Many have availed themselves of his expertise, photographs and memorabilia. As an interested observer, I could see him forming a railroad historical group here which is now a going concern.

I returned to the papers two years ago and heard they were searching for a columnist for the *San Rafael News Pointer*. "Why not Jack Farley?" I said. I knew he'd be a natural and my hunch proved correct. Meet Jack Farley author of "Station to Station" for the *San Rafael News Pointer*. A fourth generation pioneer—my old neighbor and friend.

⌐⊶⌐

To the tune of "Johnny Comes Marching Home," young Matt Thoennes, just back from the war in the Persian Gulf, was to be greeted at St. Anselm's school Tuesday by an eager fifth grade class.

The students had mailed many significant pictures and letters to the local man since last November and he planned to give back some of the encouragement they had given him. Matt was a specialist in chemical weapons who saw active combat duty in Basra, and is the son of Chuck and Carol Thoennes of San Anselmo.

The youngsters planned to sing the popular war song, placed the name Matthew where Johnny was, as well as the "Presidents March" and a vocal rendition of "The Gettysburg Address."

Matthew is one of 12 children in the Thoennes family. He attended Red Hill and Drake High School and his arrival home a week ago Sunday was the cause celebre in the town.

ooooo

Exuberance Prevailed

Exuberance prevailed as the youngsters avidly questioned the returning young solider on his activities while in combat in the Persian Gulf.

Matthew Thoennes has been the center of attention since his arrival home last week. His parents, Mr. and Mrs. Charles Thoennes, entertained for 90 at their San Anselmo home. The young man is one of 12 children and his parents are grandparents of nine as of last week. His sister gave birth in the wee hours of the night of the party.

The eager young faces of St. Anselm's fifth grade class were something to see as Matthew walked into their prepared event of songs and party welcome home. After their songs Matthew took a seat of honor while they gathered about to ask as many questions as they could of this older "brother" who was on their list of cards and letters while he was overseas.

Caroline Switzer, the class teacher, and other teachers and mothers were also present to witness what was a touching and warm welcome.

Katherine Coddington Day

It was like old home week when the San Anselmo Historical Commission met Wednesday night in the Museum.

In between reminiscences of the old days some very progressive reports were heard regarding finances, purchases and plans for the Museum staff. Also there is to be involvement in functions of related historical significance.

Karen Liberatore and Laurie Smith, co-chairpersons, addressed the fully attended meeting. Plans were made to have a speaker at the July meeting, an entry in the Country Fair Days festival in September and some participation in the 40th anniversary observance of Sir Francis Drake High School. On Country Fair Day, Preston McGinnis will drive a Rolls Royce carrying members of the Commission or other historical personages.

Tom Perry displayed an old picture of the first house built by his great-grandfather, James Ross, for whom the town of Ross was named. Perry also gave a resume of the functions of the Commission since its inception and of how gradually it is broadening to include more people.

An effort to preserve old homes and businesses to keep the old face of the town was generally noted as being successful by interested pioneers.

Barbara Jacobs, town librarian, stated that the library may still be occupied for a time as it is feasible without fear of earthquake damage.

It was learned that retiring chairperson Katharine Coddington of Ross was honored by the Town Council recently for her untiring efforts as a leader and writer in promoting history of the town. They declared June 11 to be set aside in her honor as Katherine Coddington Day.

Phil Kazan and Jack Spears were introduced as new Commission members. Others present were Bill Franchini, Bill and Jane Davis, Charles Monte, Laurie Smith, Dick McLeran, Karen Liberatore and yours truly.

Marin Birthright

Representatives of Marin's Birthright attended an international convention last week in Edmonton and Alberta, Canada. They were Margaret Farley and Donna Boyd of San Rafael.

A panel discussion on the dilemma of "Teenage Sexuality Today" was held by parents and their sons and daughters explaining why communication was so important.

The local organization at 2144 4th Street, San Rafael, now 20 years old, is a supportive service to young girls, pregnant or possibly so. Trained volunteers can give a pregnancy test, counseling and any other service desired. A hot line for troubled youth is open for 24 hours. The number is 456-4500.

More volunteers are needed in the secretarial or phone answering.

Here and There

The beautiful weather has spurred a rash of local home barbecues, etc. Bruce Hoenig has the same birthday as his year-old son, Seth. He and his wife, Melissa, and daughter, Samandhi, celebrated with a barbecue, cake, gifts and much music with family, friends and neighbors. Next door the James Turrinis were likewise entertaining family around their swimming pool.

Departure

Johnny and Rosie Stamper are leaving Marin for their new abode at Glen Haven on Clear Lake. John is a very clever jack (and even master of all trades) as well as an inventor. His wife, a native of New Zealand has been employed locally but will be further occupied up there with home and business.

Maxine Fitzgerald-Virtz, who recently moved into San Anselmo with her husband David, is to be the featured artist at the San Anselmo Public Library in July. Her artwork has been displayed through the country and coming from the Grand Tetons of Wyoming, she has some very vivid interpretations of that area as well.

ooooo

The town in the throes of a July 4th celebration in 1910. A gala that was a great occasion. Roy Farrington Jones Private Collection.

On the Merry-Go-Round

We've had an exciting merry-go-round week of attending functions with the heat wave in between.

First we went out to the Veteran's Auditorium, packed for the occasion, to enjoy the trumpet jazz of famous Al Hirt, whose specialty in Dixieland music has entertained millions for 50 years. The good old favorites were presented to an audience thirsty for artfully performed music. The Great Performances are truly brought here.

The retirees of Chevron and Standard Oil Company put on their annual "Razzle Dazzle Review" for the 19th year in the Rohnert Park Performing Arts Center. Each year it becomes an extravaganza of greater proportions entirely staged and done by the members of the "Rohnert Park Kitchen Kut-Ups." The entire program—vaudeville dances, comedy, singing and instrumentals—is done very aptly by amateurs and professionals.

On the Fourth

Of course we had to attend Marin's annual Fair out at the Veteran's Auditorium. Parking wasn't bad and the weather had cooled down from the 100 degrees.

The fine arts, photography and painting displayed the great talent we have hereabouts. Shirley De Bishop of Elm Avenue here won two first prizes with her table decoration displays; Ann Switzer of Ross achieved first place with an exquisite white dahlia painting and another San Anselman, Sherry Rice, displayed her colorful lazy quilt that brought her first honors. Little Erica Madsen of San Anselmo was very pleased that her bunny won a first.

Historical Time

Over at the Marin Historical Society's booth, it was old home week with Millie Dunshee, Warren Redding, Pat and Richard Lytel and Jack Farley. A movie on historical buildings of San Rafael was being shown.

Chris Craiker, architect and president of the Home Builders Association, was on hand to greet those interested in railroads, as we entered. The movie of the old Northwestern Pacific trains in Marin was being run while huge wall displays were done in a creative manner displaying the history of our railroads.

Was that all? No, we went to San Rafael's hit parade for the Fourth. The streets were packed with onlookers who weren't disappointed. Much honor was paid to returning veterans and airplanes overhead reminded us of the recent war. It's a happy public to see our troops home again.

Oh, yes, we ate at Denny's and drove to Tiburon to find a foggy Bay. No fireworks could be seen, so homeward bound, tired but happy over a good Fourth.

Katherine Coddington

Katherine Coddington, who recently retired from San Anselmo's Historical Commission, tells us she regrets that her life has taken a new turn. She thoroughly enjoyed teaching and sharing with people the town's history as they meandered through the local museum.

Holding a multi-subject teaching credential from Dominican College enhanced her abilities in that direction. She has a B.A. in English from Lone Mountain College, with an honor's year abroad at Oxford University. Further graduate studies were done at Stanford and S.F. State University .

She claims to have used the museum like a school bulletin board to illustrate the past with photography, textiles, cards, letters and music artifacts. In 1985 she joined the Society of California Archivists to preserve San Anselmo's stories. Her joys of writing and history were expressed in her column in the *Ross Valley Reporter* "Historical Pursuits."

Her first local publication was *The History of St. Anselm's* in August, 1982. It was then that an invitation of William Davis, chairman of the S.A. Historical Commission, began her affiliation with the local group. She found it intertwined with her academic growth. She used the museum for her writing, researching, display work, archival practice and public speaking. It opened numerous doors in her life. One thing led to another and finally her thesis project, "The Life of Frederic Lister Burk," helped her earn a master's degree in the humanities from San Francisco State. Also she published a report on the architectural heritage of San Anselmo for the State of California.

Coddington's grandparents, the late Mr. and Mrs. A.A. Coddington, were long Ross and San Anselmo pioneers. Her dad, the late Dwight Coddington, grew up here as did his siblings, Gladys, Bert and Shirley.

ooooo

The Faculty house on Bolinas Ave. built in 1920, one of the Julia Morgan (architect of the famed Hearst Castle in San Simeon) designs. San Anselmo Historical Commission.

Dog Days

Though these are dog days (that period when fleas come to life on the pets) yet what a cool summer, over all. Except for a few hot spells, we've been spared the excessive heat Marinites know so well. Lucky for us with the cinder dry landscapes already sun scorched. Mother Nature sends the cool fog drifts from the ocean saving Marin as she always has.

Famed Designer
San Anselmo homes designed by Julia Morgan of Hearst Castle fame are to be featured soon on a homes tour.

We recall our residence in San Luis Obispo during the time when my husband, Charles, a senior supervisor for the State Division of Architecture and son, Harry, then 21, were identified with the opulent castle at San Simeon. The latter worked on carving the cupolas at the top of the main building. The rambling estate and building were designed by Julia Morgan, who became responsible for over 700 structures throughout the state.

Among them were four San Anselmo homes, three in the Seminary grounds. The faculty house where Dr. Carol Robb resides is located on Bolinas Avenue. The President's house is on Seminary Road, and the theater-gymnasium is located on Kensington. Many of the community's theatricals are staged there. The "Craftsman House" owned by Paul and Elizabeth Purdon in the Barber Tract, with long side gables and varied levels, is another version of Miss Morgan's work.

Pastor Leaves
The Church of the Nazarene left San Anselmo four years ago for a Novato location close to Hamilton Field. The large sign can be seen

on the freeway. The idea was to become more accesible to the public. This proved fruitful, as many U.S. Navy couples were enabled to take advantage of the expanded church services, including the nursery.

Many of the young folks have since been transferred by the U.S. Navy to other states. Now the pastor, Rev. James Southard, is leaving for Southern California after a ten year service in Marin. He will be studying church history and soon will have a new pastorate down there. With him goes his wife, Frieda, and two young daughters, Jamie and Joanne. Frieda Southard, an R.N., is the daughter of missionaries to Nicaragua. She speaks Spanish fluently in addition to having musical abilities and special love for little children.

Sunday, a farewell luncheon followed the service with tearful goodbyes and good wishes. Among the gifts given them was a memory album with many pictures recording activities here. Stella Onizuka was chairman.

⊢━━⊣

Edward Stoner, a San Anselmo native, loves to recall the old days. He used to work for the old Cunha dairy on Butterfield Road when the glass bottles had the cream at the top. He and his friends as kids used to dam the creek in Lansdale.

ooooo

Romance in History

"San Anselmo rose to the occasion in 1979 when SAVE (San Anselmo Volunteer Effort) was founded," says Therese Stawowy. Now with recession here again and technological changes, Mrs. Stawowy claims a great need is there for volunteers to subsidize many town activities. This was brought to the attention of the San Anselmo Historical Commission Wednesday in the Museum.

Needs of the Public

Duties to be filled range from bulb planting to research, helping the handicapped, docent recruitment and schools, home and community service. In 1980 a seven member board was appointed with Mrs. Stawowy joining as leader in 1983. The board set up a phone and disaster system after the 1982 flood. In 1984 SAVE came under the town administration.

SAVE now recruits volunteers to staff the museum and others will act as docents for tour walks. Mrs. Stawowy, a former teacher and school administrator, claims that people are a town's greatest resource. There are openings to suit all who volunteer. She listed the many accomplishments of SAVE and stated the friends of SAVE have bought a computer for the data bank. She also announced the theme for San Anselmo Country Fair Days in September to be Mardi Gras.

Other Reports

The meeting was conducted by Laurie Smith and Karen Liberatore, co-chairwomen. Ms. Smith reported on a meeting held at Seminary here with their staff members, Adele Anthony, Michael Petersen and Lucky Phelps, along with Pat Hensen of the Commission.

Mrs. Hensen, chairman of the annual Commission dinner on

October 16 at the Seminary, is hoping for an even larger attendance of those interested in San Anselmo's history for this event. A delicious dinner is served and an excellent program planned for old and new residents who wish to find out more about the town's early years. Mrs. Hensen, herself a history teacher at Sonoma State University, reported on the extensive retrofitting being planned for Seminary buildings, especially Montgomery Chapel with an $8 million budget on remodeling costs.

The San Francisco Presbyterian Theological Seminary contains San Anselmo's pioneer structures having begun here in 1874. Its buildings and lovely trees have blended well. Sitting like castles amidst San Anselmo's hills, it contributes a romantic and European look as one views the town.

Chuck Hensen reported on the data base that he and Tom Perry are conferring over, i.e., records of homes, photos and dates. The museum will then be able to project information to the visitor on a more specific basis.

B. Dayz

This week the families joined me for a birthday observance. Pat Nielsen and family came from Atlanta and we had lunch in Petaluma with brother John O'Brien, and Alice Brown Monte, my sister-in-law. There was a cousin visit with Buzz Brown and Charles Monte. Then the Willits family joined us and later April and Steve Lynn from Oakley. Dave and Jan, Mt. Shasta fishing guides, are up there carefully watching the Sacto River weed killer spill. That section is under ecological ruin, but Lake Shasta is an immense body of water with five rivers leading into it so there is more hope there. Dave and Jan are real lovers of the land and seldom keep a fish but release it soon after its caught. The tragedy has affected the entire region and beyond as nature is destroyed by man-made units.

Making Waves

Redwood Empire Waves Unit 77 celebrated its second birthday with a gathering of the members at Novato Saturday. The new unit is open to all who have been in the Waves. The national organization is now 50 years old.

Members present to enjoy the birthday cake and reminisce about the old war days were Rita Davidson, B. Ann Bragg, Charlotte Kelly, Claire Grubbs, Helen Hartley, Ann Fried, Rena Suberg, Bettie Crandall, Fran Trouette, Barbara McArther, Clara Stoner and Edwina Cann.

ooooo

The James Taylor (son of Samuel P. Taylor) home built in Victorian Chinoiserie style in 1895. The Samuel Taylor Park in Lagunitas Creek is a fine memorial. San Anselmo Historical Commission.

Theatrics and Great Art

Theatrics and great art have been on our agenda for this week. It's all so cultural and within short driving distance. Fine for keeping the minds off of the weird weather and happenings. Thank God for the rain!

Last week we visited the De Young Museum in Golden Gate Park to view the works of Albert Bierstadt (1830-1902), prominent landscape painter whose early panoramic renditions of the Rockies, the Sierras and Yosemite are heroic. In his youth his talent wasn't recognized, but he continued studying. A century later, a collection of 70 of his finest paintings from the Brooklyn Museum are leaving thousands in breathless awe.

The exhibit is open to the public Wednesday through Sunday mornings and ends on September 1. It is closed Monday and Tuesdays. The handicapped are welcomed and accommodated with wheelchairs available.

A Tragic Side

There was a tragic side to the Samuel Taylor story. Samuel, who built the first paper mill on this coast, made a great success until the mogul William Coleman of San Rafael bought some water rights from him and the mill ran out of water. He died, and his widow, Sarah, tried to recoup but borrowed money she couldn't repay as a depression hit. She was not allowed to return there, even after death. She died at the home of her son, William, in San Anselmo. William and brother James, two of the Taylor's seven sons, bought land on the San Anselmo creek and built a home in 1895, which still stands. It is a Victorian incorporating Chinese styling. James became a state assemblyman after beginning as a San Anselmo trustee, while his brother, William, served as a Marin sheriff. Their mother, Sarah

Irving Taylor, was related to Washington Irving.

However, the connection to Sleepy Hollow stops there. One of the Hotaling family named the area when he arranged for his Bohemian Club friends to go hunting in the valley.

Anyway, Samuel P. Taylor's name is now a living landmark with a state park named for him and giving pleasure to many thousands through the years.

They Did It Again

A performance fit for kings was the Ross Valley Players' last rendition of the "Cabaret International" at The Barn in the Marin Art and Garden Center in Ross.

The musical comedy had songs of Gershwin, Berlin, Hammerstein and Sondheim that were never better rendered. A very talented pianist, Jim Lahti, wasn't the least of it, further enhancing the show with his artistry. I had him autograph my program. His wife, Mary, was a song and dance person in the show. The cast, all locals, were very professional.

A New Switch

Jack Eisen was a San Rafael High School boy who used to love the old *Marin Journal* (weekly) office when I was the society editor there many years ago. In fact the old *Journal* published his first story on commute transportation when he was 16 years old. From there he went on to a 45-year career of news writing, including being a columnist for the noted *Washington Post* for 30 years. Now in retirement, he is editing the *Headlight*, news organ for the Northwestern Pacific Railroad Historical Society.

He writes a column called the "Whistling Post." In the last edition he mentions reading this column's story of the Farley family in San Rafael. He was tickled over the fact that I called the son, little Jackie, as Jack Farley is the membership chairman of the organization, and as he says, he expanded from that description. He mentions he also is not able to throw darts. He says after his story written 50 years ago was published, some stuff hit the fan. Sorry, Jack Eisen, I can't recall that but maybe you can refresh my memory.

I have movies of Jack Junior playing in our backyard with our famous "Bonzo." Jack Farley has had much acclaim for his historical column "Station to Station" in the *San Rafael News Pointer*. Our dog, Bonzo, has become famous due to his true Bonzo dog stories. That dog was a character, shared by our neighbors, spoiled by our grandmothers and given train rides by conductor Walter Howe, who carried a good supply of bones. Animals aren't perfect but they are close to humans.

ooooo

Since 1874 San Anselmo has had as a dominant landmark the San Francisco Presbyterian Theological Seminary. Pictured is Montgomery Chapel and adjoining buildings before century's turn. Roy Farrington Jones Private Library.

Historical Events

San Anselmo remains warmer due to its protective hills, consequently my harvest was just great, pears and tomatoes, juicy and prolific, in a protected area. However, the summer was a bummer and Indian summer days are usually real hot.

Meanwhile the old Cary house at the top of Redwood Avenue is being readied for guests on Sunday. They'll be coming up the hill by van from the Seminary's Montgomery Chapel fundraiser on that day. Maryanne Cowperthwaite, whose family has been long identified with San Anselmo and the Seminary, is involved with the event. This precedes by one day the annual dinner of the San Anselmo Historical Commission at the Seminary dining area. Pat Hensen, a history teacher at Sonoma State, her husband, Chuck, and Laurie Smith are active in the plans.

Montgomery Chapel was built in 1874 at the foot of Seminary Hill for a chapel and mausoleum for the body of Alexander Montgomery, a Scotch-Irishman, and chief benefactor of the Presbyterian Church. The chapel, built with stones from local quarries, stands at the corner of Richmond Road and Bolinas Avenue here. In the century's early days it was used as a backdrop for silent movies, due to its Romanesque architecture.

Mardi Gras

Don't forget September 22 for the gala San Anselmo fete when the town will be turned into a "Mardi Gras." This will be fun for all ages. History will be dispensed with historical brochures, etc. in the local historical booth. SAVE volunteers are helping with the booths' construction.

We guided visitors through San Francisco sites last week on their first trip here. At Fisherman's Wharf they marveled at the dungeness crab at Castagnolas, listened to the street musicians and watched artists at cannery row. One character, the strawman, scared people by jumping as they walked by and amused the crowd. A large sea lion followed the returning fishing boats while pelicans waited patiently to be fed. We went through the Haight-Ashbury, then Golden Gate Park and the Japanese gardens. At Shrader Street we found a little known hill at the top and sat on rocks marveling at the panoramic view of the city, the Bay and the bridges. Unbeatable!

Dr. Frank Keegan of the Marin Chamber of Commerce, who is writing a book on Marin history asked Bill Davis, our local history commissioner, for leading events in San Anselmo history. Listed were: 1874—railroad begins operation; 1892—Seminary erected; 1906—influx of residents; 1907—town incorporation; and 1982—major flood.

It's Thirty

The 95-year-old *Mill Valley Record* passed from the scene this week as well as the popular *Coastal Post*, dependable for its truth. Cause—poor advertising. The notable news term "thirty" for a record of performance that shouldn't be forgotten. Lucretia Hansen, late editor of the *Record*, was herself an institution and Don Deane, of the *Post*, a brave man.

Gay and Sandie Verdon, the mother daughter duo, that have operated the Pet Food Cottage for 12 years, celebrated Valentine's Day with an artistic display of pets done by San Anselmo photographer Dondelot.

It was to "honor the love between people and their pets" and includes matted and framed prints of cats, dogs and horses. Ms. Dondelot had won prizes for these prints. They include "Caught Napping," "Curiosity," "Majesty," "Playful" and "Sweet Taste of Victory".

The Pet Food Cottage is a San Anselmo landmark having been established since 1939 and is located at 326 San Anselmo Avenue.

The Verdons are both owners of numerous dogs and cats and are truly animal lovers.

ooooo

Old Major and Colonel, original fire horses of the San Anselmo Fire Deportment pulling the old fire wagon with firemen dressed in their finest. Marty Marcucci Collection.

Teacher Par Excellence

❧ Our wildlife are suffering from the drought as all of our yard's water receptacles are drained nightly. We'll just have to put out more as they have to drink too. This year's Indian summer is prefaced by cool, overcast mornings and blasting hot afternoons in the 90's. Is there no happy medium?

※

Old Major and Colonel, the fire horses that pulled San Anselmo's wagon to many a fire—with Chief Cartright—had a hard time when the City bought the first fire engine. Showing up at many fires by habit, they were finally farmed out to graze quietly—all the fun gone from their lives.

※

Doesn't everybody remember Gladys Kenney Hodgson, dance teacher par excellence, with studios that still bear her name down on Tunstead Avenue here? Over a 50-year period she taught thousands of Marin girls ballet at a nominal price because of her humanitarian outlook.

Born and raised in Santa Rosa where her father was a dance teacher, Gladys had a career as a prima ballerina before settling down in Ross with her husband, Ralston Hodgson. She had taught me and a group of Ross schoolgirls to do the Minuet at an early Grape Festival on the Kent Estate. Later my daughter was in her classes in San Anselmo, so Gladys had carried on faithfully for many years. During the later time the annual Ballet-Aquacade was started by her and became a smashing success with thousands of dollars donated to hospitals for necessary medical equipment. It was so perfected by Gladys, with Minnie Cuneo of San Anselmo supervising the costumes, that it became Marin's leading event for all to see for a charitable cause. Youngsters from five through teenage participated. One of the stars was Betty Cuneo (now Mrs. Robert Alvarado of San Anselmo). Betty then became an assistant teacher and on Gladys' demise took over the School of the Dance. She retired one year ago and it is now directed by Allison Adams. Betty and Gladys were teaching together for 30 years.

Dr. Scott Polland's widow, Jean, who with her sister, Marian Hall resides at Villa Marin loved to recall those days when their three daughters, Jeanie, Peggy and Marion took part in the ballet and extravaganza. Another was Patty Chapman, daughter of the Roland Chapmans of Ross.

Mrs. Hodgson passed away several years ago, leaving two daughters, Marcia and Sandy and several grandchildren. Her untiring efforts in serving youth of the area for many years are not forgotten and remain as a part of their lives.

⋈

Hundreds of women from local churches attended the interdenominational retreat of the Women of Christ (WIC) in Santa Rosa's Flamingo Hotel over the weekend.

Four speakers from all walks of life informed them of how Christ has entered their tragic lives and performed miracles. Carol Matrisciana had a jet set life but found it disappointing. With her husband, Patrick, they now produce videos exposing pagan influences in our society. Carol Selander, overcoming incest and anorexia, became a noted leader and pastor's wife with counseling degrees. Jen Gregory was an incest victim and bulemic before finding the Lord and is now a minister and completing a nursing degree. Jan Walker, a music minister in Richmond, was told she wasn't college material. Her excellent grades and degrees from University of California, Berkeley proved differently. Her demands are many as a speaker and singer.

Patty Weaver and Denise Howard of Novato interspersed their songs with the speakers and brought down the house with their fervency.

Maggie Ricciardi and Carol Bell of Novato arranged the event and counselors were Caroline and Steve Morris of Kentfield, Susan

Burkout of Corte Madera, Martha Saul of Mill Valley and Tom Swanson of San Rafael.

ooooo

William Rattray of Ross awaits at San Anselmo Railroad Station for guests, about 1900. May-Murdock Publications.

Marin as It Was

A bit of old Ross-San Anselmo is still intact as well as the families who've lived there for four generations.

We've been reading the bio of Jayne Rattray Murdock and it sounds so much like my own in the early days here when we had so much freedom as children.

Jayne and her husband Dick Murdock, a columnist for a local daily, have just published their 15th book and are still residing in her old family home on Glenwood Avenue in Ross. It had been the place originally of her parents, Bill and Marian Rattray, long identified with Marin's social and civic life. Bill was a concert pianist and gave his talent to his church, St. John's in Ross, the Marin Music Chest and was always available for other groups (including Gladys Kenney Hodgson's School of the Dance located on Tunstead Avenue).

Music Chest Formed

It was about 1932 when the Marin Music Chest was formed to provide top music to all of Marin for an entrance fee of 25 cents. Retired opera star, Maud Fay Symington, was the originator; Kitty Oppenheimer, the publicist; and Marian and Bill Rattray were general managers. Jayne reminded us that her parents kept the receipts of the concerts under their bed until the banks opened on Monday.

Nelson Eddy, scheduled to perform at a concert at the Fairfax Pavilion was suddenly taken with stomach cramps. Marian Rattray brewed him some tea and with TLC, he was able to perform. Bill, who was a fine pianist, was often pressed into duty on the stage at Forest Meadows at Dominican to keep the sheet music from being blown away. In 1942 he was the soloist with Marin Symphony, playing a Saint Saen concerto, being very well received.

Marian headed the Red Cross Canteen during WWI serving food to the servicemen going through Hamilton Field. After the war she became executive director of the Marin Chapter of Red Cross until 1959. Born in Alameda in 1894, Marian died in the Ross home in 1976, one of Hospice of Marin's first patients. Jayne wrote a book about caring for her mother in her last days. Bill was born in Oakland in 1892 and succumbed in a Novato nursing home in 1964. They had been married in June 1917 just weeks after she had graduated from Mills college. Marian's parents, George and Susan Murdock, built a summer home on Austin Avenue here in 1904. Susan was a college grad, a rare feat in those days. Marian at age nine planted the now towering redwood tree on the west side of the front yard.

Co-authors

Jayne a graduate of Ross School, Tamalpais High and U.C. Berkeley later received her teaching degree and taught in Mill Valley. She was always a writer and after two husbands and five children, met her present husband, Dick Murdock, who had been a locomotive engineer on the trains in Dunsmuir. His books *Smoke in the Canyon* and *Love Affair with Steam* were very successful beginners to a sequel of books later published with Jayne, like *Point Bonita to Point Reyes* and the newest *Lime Point to Lawson's Landing*.

Her son, Bruce Cozzi, resides on the Ross estate with his family who attend the Ross School. Jayne has four other grown children and many grandchildren. She is currently writing about her family in Ross. Dick is writing about a famous railroad person. They both lead seminars throughout the Bay Area on fishing, publishing and railroading and operate the May-Murdock publications in Ross.

Sense of History

As part of the Heritage program for Ross Valley schools, I was privileged to talk on the local history to a group of students at Wade Thomas School here. It was like going home for me as my "children" David, Pat and Harry were graduates of the school during which time I served as publicity chairman for the P.T.A.

Pupils from Mrs. Glasman's second grade and from Mrs. Sweeting's fifth grade were a very intrigued audience and pictures of the flood of '82 in San Anselmo drew many questions. Jeni Foote, assistant student teacher, coordinated the program.

85 Years

The San Anselmo Historical Commission at its recent meeting made preliminary announcements of their part in San Anselmo's 85th birthday celebration. According to Laurie Smith, co-chair of the group, there is a slide show of old prints being planned by Pat Swensen, who is working with the Seminary librarian on this. The date is to be April 9 as San Anselmo formal town beginnings were on that date in 1907. Therese Stawowy, of SAVE (San Anselmo Volunteer Effort) is discussing plans with local Chamber of Commerce President Holly Spint and administrator Connie Rogers.

〜

I do have some collections of pictures, books and memorabilia that would do very well in a museum or historical place for all to see.

My collection of vintage pictures includes one of a very stately gentleman, my great-grandfather, with white hair, goatee and a handsome black suit with velvet lapels. A good humored face belies the stern visage. His stately hands rest on his knee and the table next to him. On the back of the picture it says Leonard Purley Smith, mayor of Seattle, 1880-1882. It was taken in California about 1883. With his family he left Bangor, Maine to travel around the Horn going west. He had been in the Maine legislature. The family went into Colusa, California before traveling to Seattle, where he became the city's first mayor. With his son, Alfred Alcott Smith, he later owned a large jewelry store in Seattle.

ooooo

Domingo Sais and his wife about 1840. San Anselmo Historical Commission.

A Little Spanish Town

The early Spanish land grants in this area hold a fascination for me as my own grandmother was holder of a San Diego grant. Ours was later destroyed in the Seattle waterfront fire, so all we could claim was her physical heritage, which mixed with the Irish, turned out some beauties.

Domingo Sais, whose father was a soldier in Monterey in 1782, first came to a Marin shore on a raft floating from the Presidio to Big Rock off Point San Quentin. His own first dwelling was built of tulles gathered from a pond located where Yolansdale is right now. In return for military service and as a public official he was granted two square leagues. He called the grant Cañada de Herrera (vale of the blacksmiths) and it included what is now San Anselmo and Fairfax.

The hillsides had redwoods and oaks and the valley was fertile. Domingo's second house, a large hacienda on the south side of Sir Francis Drake, was where he brought wife and family. Built of adobe brick, it was named "Al Pavidion." He devoted his time to stocking his rancho with cattle, horses and sheep, tilling the valley to raise food for his family and stock. His large family assisted as they grew older. They entertained in the Hispanic way with fiestas inviting all who could come.

Fairfax, Too

A 40-acre tract was deeded by the Sais heirs to Charles S. Fairfax, a descendant of English barons and his wife who was a niece of Senator John C. Calhoun. The happy days at the Hacienda were ended with the death of Domingo Sais, killed by a fall from a horse in 1853. His widow owned the original Fairfax park and rented out 65 acres for picnics.

The heirs included six children and no will was made. Ten years after his death the estate was probated, but much confusion existed as many children were getting married.

Three avenues remain as reminders of these pioneers. Domingo in Fairfax; Sais and Camina de Herrera Avenues in San Anselmo. A vast number of descendants remain, many of whom became popular and well known in the area.

70-Year Celebration

A large-celebration for St. Anselm's Y.L.I. 70th year of organization was an impressive one recently at the church social hall here.

Visitors from other institutes in the state numbered about 50 as a delightful repast and program were presented to mark the many years the church's ladies' group has been operating.

Co-chairwomen were Helen Benz and Loretta O'Rourke, who is a past grand president.

〜

San Anselmo's Historical Commission is burgeoning and plans are to enlarge with an auxiliary group. This would be similar to the Friends of the Library which has been so effective.

Presiding over a fully attended session Wednesday night were the co-chairpersons Karen Liberatore and Laurie Smith. A series of interesting plans for the future were discussed.

Donations of pictures and artifacts given by town's pioneers were acknowledged. The importance of keeping the old face of town intact was stressed. Many of the architectural facades are irreplaceable in impressions to those residents and visitors.

Heather Lamb, co-librarian of the San Anselmo Public Library, reported on the progress made with the local library building. An engineer consultant, John Hill, is currently working with the town administrator on this project.

ooooo

Busy Retirement

Alan Creighton, San Anselmo pioneer, was on TV last week describing his work with the historic tug "Hercules" in restoration at Sausalito Bay Center.

The tug was built on the east coast in 1908, sailed west through the Magellen Straights before the Panama Canal to live an active life on this coast. It is now under jurisdiction of the Department of the Interior and is near the historic lumber schooner "Wapama" located atop a barge near Harbor Drive. It is on view to the public on Saturday at the Sausalito Bay Model where park rangers conduct guided tours.

Used Abilities

Creighton, a Sausalito native, is a retired fireman and engineer of the old Sausalito ferries as well as a state certified steam boiler inspector. His interest and expertise in the tug's care is of importance. His parents, the late Edward and Loretta Creighton, came to Sausalito from San Francisco in 1907 and moved to Tiburon to raise their six children, of whom four survive. All attended Tamalpais High School and Al and wife, Dorothy, resided in Mill Valley for 15 years before coming here 40 years ago.

Their sons are Dick Creighton, Spanish teacher at Drake High School; Greg Creighton, construction estimator in Chico, and the late David Creighton of San Anselmo. They have ten grandchildren, so Al keeps busy with his membership on the San Anselmo Historical Commission, his family and historical interests.

History Book

It all began last month with a story of Dick and Jayne Murdock, the publishers who lead the Marin Small Publishers Association. I attended one of their meetings and caught on listening to the stories given by many self-publishing authors. They were writing and publishing about everything. One book written by a mother who lost her son was entitled *Is There Life After Grief?* It gave recovery practices for the grief-stricken. One young lady wanted to publish a cookbook to raise funds for the Marin Concerned Citizens to aid the homeless.

So coming in February, my column "Tracks from the Junction" will officially appear in a book by that name and the locals and everyone who has enjoyed it will be able to have one. It's not a big money making item, so I'm not going to make a fortune.

Originally, Cinda Becker, who deserves credit for the name and purpose to chronicle historical anecdotes, gave me the job. She had come to interview me about the demise of my late husband, Charles Brown, and left informing me of my new capacity. It's been fun for me and the columns are now being computed, readied for the designing by Janet Andrews of Larkspur.

ooooo

Order Form

Marin Light Press
81 Elm Avenue
San Anselmo, CA 94960

Please send the following number of books: _____
Price per book is $18.95
Total cost of selected number of books: _____

Shipping $2.00 first book _____
$1.00 each additional book

Please add 7.25% sales tax if reside in Calif. _____

Total amount for books, shipping and sales tax _____

_____

_____

_____

ɔney order payable to:

ɔ period of 3 to 4 weeks for delivery.

Thank you